A *Highland* Autumn

Sophia Nye

Other Books By Sophia Nye

Seasons of Scotland

Grab a cup of tea, fall into your favorite armchair, and fall in love with a cast of larger-than-life characters on their spirited misadventures.
Seasons of Scotland follows the story of three Highland clans over the course of one year as they face the political turmoil of twelfth-century Scotland, all while their warriors are busy falling head-over-heels in love.
From poorly planned escapes to murder attempts and everything in between, it's lucky for our band of Highlanders and their lasses that love does indeed conquer all.

To Love A Laird
Alec & Nora's Story
Available exclusively to newsletter subscribers

A Highland Autumn
Ronan & Adelina's Story

A Wild Winter
Aidan & Gemma's Story

A Scandalous Spring
Fintan & Sybilla's Story

A Sizzling Summer
Donnan & Deirdre's Story

Each book in the Seasons of Scotland series can be read in order or as a standalone novel.

A Highland Autumn
Seasons of Scotland Book 1
Sophia Nye

Cover by Dar Albert

First Edition published October 2020

For Cole -
The only journey worth taking is the one I take with you.

PROLOGUE

October 17, 1136

Filtered moonlight illuminated the muddy forest path. 'Twas a full moon, bright and silver behind the canopy above. Wind whistled through the shaking trees, and Ewan could feel the dampness of midnight settling in his bones. The rain would begin soon. He'd already been on the road for three days, riding fast and hard for as long as his horse could manage it. Every second counted – a man's life depended upon him.

By tomorrow night, he would arrive at Calder Keep with an urgent letter for Laird Murdoch Calder. He'd been told the message verbally, aye, but he also carried a secret missive, hidden beneath the folds of his plaid. 'Twas not in the sort of place you'd normally keep belongings, so that if anything were to happen there was still a chance that the laird would be warned in time.

Exhaustion crept slowly through his body, threatening to slow him down. He paused for just a moment, resting his head on the wiry mane of his horse. Leaves rustled. Not in the trees, but somewhere on the ground. Somewhere nearby. The horse's ears twitched outward. He'd heard it, too.

'Twas likely a rabbit, Ewan decided. His foggy mind was surely playing tricks on him. Not much longer, and he'd be able to rest. Until then, he needed to keep going.

A twig snapped. Something was in the brush a stone's throw from him.

Chills ran down his back. His heart hammered in his chest, and Ewan drew his greatsword. Lord, let it be a rabbit.

The bushes in front of him shook and creaked. 'Twas no rabbit. Instead, a woman wearing a long, hooded cloak stumbled onto the path.

Ewan sighed in relief, sheathing his sword and offering his arm to steady her. "Are ye lost, lass?" he asked, trying to make out a face beneath her deep hood.

"Oh, aye," she answered. "Where does this road lead?"

"This is the road to Calder lands," he replied. "Where are ye headed?"

"That's where I'll be going," she said. "Are you going that way as well?"

Ewan could hear the hope in her voice. The poor lass must be wanting for company through the night. He could hardly blame her. Though the Calder laird kept his lands safer than most, brigands had a way of getting around guards. One could never be too careful.

"Aye," Ewan said, "but I'll be traveling in haste. You're welcome to come along if ye can keep up."

She hesitated, looking up and down the empty road. Wringing her hands nervously, she looked toward him, shrouded in the darkness of her cloak. "I'm not alone," she admitted. "I've a wee lad waiting for me to tell him 'tis safe. Could you spare a moment to help me retrieve him? I've no doubt we can keep up with you then."

A sense of urgency told Ewan he shouldn't linger. He should pick up his pace and leave the lass to make her own way. A sense of decency and compassion wouldn't allow him to do so.

"Please," the woman begged.

Ewan groaned in frustration. "We must be quick," he said. "I've already rested far too long."

The woman turned and headed back through the bush behind her. Ewan followed her moments later.

"Surely you could afford a short respite," she commented as they walked through the underbrush. "No journey is so urgent you need to tire yourself."

"I wish that were the truth, lass," Ewan said, "but 'tis not."

"What requires such haste?" she asked, passing behind a large oak.

"I carry a message for Laird Calder," he told her. He stopped speaking instantly, realizing he had already said too much. He'd been warned not to speak of his message to anyone. Likely that warning applied doubly to cloaked women wandering alone at midnight in the woods. Ewan decided this entire conversation had been a mistake. He needed to get away from the lass before he said anything else better kept secret.

"Have no fear," she called, stopping to face him. "I won't tell anyone of the assassin sent to kill the laird."

Ewan's stomach flipped over, a sick sense of foreboding returning tenfold. "I didn't tell ye that," he stated. "Who are ye?"

The woman took a step toward him, and Ewan wondered a moment too late if he should draw his sword. Her dagger slid between his ribs before he let out another breath.

She whispered into his ear as he slid to the forest floor. "I'm the assassin."

Chapter One

September 23, 1136

"Why is Cicero doing this to me? Why!" Jocelin, her older brother, shouted before falling backward onto his pillow.

"Cicero's been dead for centuries, Jo. You're the one doing the wronging," Adelina said as calmly as she could manage. "He's probably rolling over in his grave." She pressed her fingers to her temples, hoping that might afford her the patience to explain the sentence to her brother one more time.

"Alright, fine," he said, sitting up and staring at her with wide, bloodshot eyes. "I understand that the words are out of order. I get it. But *why*? Why on earth confuse people like that? How does it improve his speech?"

God bless Jocelin and his enduring practicality. Oh, he knew every word of Latin ever spoken to him. But the intricacies of rhetoric? He thought them nothing more than an oddly deliberate mistake. Adelina had been helping him with his studies for hours now in preparation for his exams in the morning. She was willing to give him one more try before she gave up and moved on to something more stimulating.

"He did it to get your attention, Jo. And it worked, didn't it? Here you are talking about three stupid words that you would have otherwise read right over. You, and every Roman who listened to that speech."

His eyes widened even more, if that were possible, and brightened up a bit. Finally, he understood enough to pass, she hoped. But that was more than enough of Cicero. Adelina stood from the chair she had been sitting in and stretched.

"You're not leaving yet, are you?" Jocelin whined.

"Jo, you'll do fine," she soothed. "I need some air." Adelina hurried toward the door to make her escape.

"I think they'll let you in soon," he said.

Adelina froze. She had applied for the third time to take courses with her brother at Oxford. All the masters knew she studied alongside him in the evenings, but until she was given formal permission, she couldn't sit in on the lectures. Jo was likely just baiting her back in to help him, but her curiosity was piqued.

"Have you heard something?" she asked, spinning around in the doorway to face him.

He smiled but said nothing.

"Jo," Adelina whined, "what did they say?"

He continued smiling, whilst making a ridiculous face. Still no comment.

"Jo!" she shouted.

He burst into laughter, but finally gave in. "They told me to have you and father go to Master Gregory's home tomorrow morning, before lectures begin."

Adelina squeaked and bounded over to hug her brother. When they had rejected her the last two times, it was in writing. The masters had never once asked to meet with her. Hope welled within her, and Adelina had to force herself not to get too excited. Nothing would be worse than yet another rejection, and in person no less.

"Did you tell father yet?" she asked, unable to stop smiling.

"Aye, I knew he'd be abed before we finished our studies. He was just as happy as you are," Jocelin answered.

"Well how did they seem when they spoke with you? Were they smiling or frowning? Who did you speak with?" Adelina couldn't keep the questions from spilling out.

Jocelin put his hand on her face to physically stop her from speaking.

"Addi, you'll be just fine. Don't you start fretting already," he said, taking his hand away. "If they meant to reject you again, why wouldn't they simply deliver another letter?"

That had been her thinking as well, yet it seemed so dangerous to hope for anything other than rejection. She could hardly believe she might at last be able to attend lectures with her brother, instead of relying on his retellings of them.

Jocelin saw the direction her thoughts were going and came to her rescue.

"Go on," he said, pushing her out the door. "Enough of schooling your dim-witted brother in rhetoric. Go find that friend of yours and take your mind off the matter."

"Gemma," Adelina said, at the same moment Jocelin closed the door behind her. "Her name is Gemma."

A few weeks ago, the girls had become fast friends at the university's library. Gemma was a skilled healer, but unable to read in Latin, making it difficult for her to study the classical medical works written by ancient authors like Dioscorides. Adelina knew nothing about herb lore and medicine, but could read Latin as well as any Oxford student. A quick deal later, Adelina was learning about the healing arts and Gemma was learning how to read Latin. Though she probably could have asked for payment in exchange for the lessons, Adelina found that information was almost always more useful than coin.

Not to mention that of all the things Adelina lacked, money wasn't one of them. Her father, Henry Matheson, had amassed a fortune by building a trading business over the last thirty-odd years. Adelina and her brother had received the best education money could buy, and many of the opportunities that afforded. There was only one thing holding Adelina back: her lack of noble heritage.

Jocelin's future was bright, even without a noble title or backing. With an Oxford education and nearly limitless funding, he could do just about anything. Adelina, as a woman, truly needed the extra status that nobility would give her to accomplish her dreams. Had she been a noble, the masters would have admitted her already. It seemed she was doomed to live a life in the shadows of girls born into a noble heritage. Always beside them, but never a peer.

She found Gemma in a small forest just outside of the town of Oxford. Adelina was not a large woman. In fact, she was on the smaller side of average in height. Next to Gemma's petite frame, however, she felt like a giant. When she located Gemma in the woods, her friend had been nearly engulfed in a wild blackberry bush. Gemma's arrow-straight black hair was all Adelina could see poking out from the bramble.

"What are we up to this evening?" Adelina asked, startling Gemma.

"Heavens, Addi," she said, putting her hand dramatically to her chest, "I thought the Devil himself had snuck up on me."

"Michaelmas isn't for a few more weeks yet," Adelina reminded her with a grin, "I think you're alright in the blackberries tonight."

Adelina tied up her long skirts to form a pocket and stepped up to the bush to pick berries. A few more made it into her mouth than her skirts, but Gemma seemed none the wiser. Adelina looked at her friend, quiet and focused on her gathering, before she realized that Gemma wasn't picking only berries. She was also grabbing handfuls of leaves.

"What are you doing?" Adelina asked.

Gemma looked at her, and then noticed her staring at the leaves in her hands. "The leaves have as many uses as the berries," she offered in answer, "and they last much longer after picking."

"What do you do with them?" Adelina took every opportunity to ply her friend for knowledge. Gemma was the best healer in the north of England. Once she made her way through some of those old medical tracts, Gemma might very well be the best healer in all of England.

"What are they called?" Gemma shot right back with a no-nonsense look and a sugary smile.

Adelina laughed. She should've known better.

"Rubus," Adelina answered her. "Rubus is a blackberry bush."

"You're not going to like my answer," Gemma said matter-of-factly.

"Well aren't we presumptuous," Adelina retorted. "I'll just be happy to know anything about it."

Gemma grimaced. "That's the trick of it," she said, "I know some things that it does, but I'm not certain why just yet."

"What on earth does that even mean?" Adelina asked, turning to face her and halting her blackberry picking.

"Well," Gemma began tentatively, "salves made from leaves or berries help with dry or irritated skin. And the leaves and berries can be eaten or drunk in an infusion to help with maladies of the mouth, throat, and stomach. Particularly where there's irritation or a rash or some such trouble."

"That's good to know," Adelina replied encouragingly. "I don't know why you thought that wouldn't be helpful."

"That's not all," Gemma continued. "There are a handful of plants that I call miracle plants. Every once in a while, I come across a sickness I can't identify. If the patient appears ill from something internal, and I can't tell what it is, I have them consume those plants. Blackberries are one of them. Something about them just helps. You'll laugh," she added as an afterthought, "but I even give them to patients with head injuries. If the centers of the eyes aren't expanding and contracting when light hits them, blackberries always help. Don't ask me why."

Adelina frowned. "Ugh, Gemma, what am I to do with that? Throw blackberries at the unsuspecting public?"

"If you're lucky, you won't be anywhere near the unsuspecting public without me until you've had a good deal more practice," Gemma said.

Adelina suddenly remembered the news that she had yet to share with her friend. Excitement struck her all over again, and she jumped up onto her toes, nearly spilling the blackberries from her skirts. Gemma raised an eyebrow but said nothing. She knew Adelina wouldn't be quiet for long.

"Oh, Gemma! I almost forgot! You'll never guess what Jo told me," she squealed. She didn't wait for Gemma to guess. How could she? It was too exciting. "I'm to meet with the masters tomorrow morning! They want to speak with me!"

"Do you think they're going to admit you?" Gemma asked.

"They've never asked to meet with me before. What else could it be?" Adelina replied.

"Adelina, have you considered what this means? If they let you in, you'll be the first woman to ever take classes as a student at Oxford."

Adelina thought about that. She rather liked the sound of being the first woman into Oxford, and not even noble-born at that. Oh, yes, Adelina had a good feeling about it. Tomorrow, something amazing was going to happen, she just knew it.

Chapter Two

September 20, 1136

Their horse's hoof beats thundered across a sea of fading grass. Sólas, his black destrier, reveled in the exercise as Ronan turned to look at his riding companion and man-at-arms, Fintan. His infectious grin of pure joy at the ride soon had Ronan smiling as well.

"It never ceases to amaze me that you take so much joy from a daily chore," Ronan commented, scanning the approaching line of mountains for signs of raiders.

"Aye, and it never ceases to amaze me that you can be so grim all the time," Fintan retorted, his grin widening at his jibe.

Ronan rolled his eyes, but returned them quickly to the places he knew made an ambush far too easy. The fall months were some of the most dangerous for the cattle droves. While they were moving the herds from the summer pasture down to winter shelters, raiders from neighboring clans need but find the right spot and they had an easy steal. Ronan rode the rough roads between Calder Keep and the summer pastures every few days to ensure the drovers didn't run into too much trouble. They had enough on their hands keeping track of the beasts.

"I don't see a thing," Fintan said after he, too, scanned the horizon. "I doubt we'll have any trouble from now 'til sundown."

Ronan nodded, slowing his horse so he could have a rest. "Aye," he agreed, "but I still have an odd feeling. Something's off today."

Then he heard it. A rider. But not from the mountains. Nay, 'twas approaching from behind them. Both warriors turned about-face, ready to draw swords at a moment's notice.

Fintan recognized the messenger first. "Looks like you have your answer," he said, "Something's off back at home."

Ronan grimaced. He knew, with painful certainty, what was coming. Watching the messenger approach, he said a silent prayer that he was wrong. It went unanswered.

"Your father wants to see you straightaway," the messenger shouted when he was within earshot. Without awaiting a reply, he turned and headed straight back toward Calder Keep.

Ronan fought the pang of annoyance. 'Twas not a convenient time to demand his presence, and his father knew it. What was more, Ronan knew exactly what his father wanted. Every time he summoned Ronan with all urgency, it meant he'd chosen a new potential bride to convince him to marry. Fintan would have to finish the cattle drive without him today. Urging his horse forward with a groan of despair, Ronan left to answer his father's summons.

Ronan stormed into the cold, gray keep. A weaker man would have struggled to open the heavy oaken doors while battling the Highland winds. Ronan, in his great anger, threw them open wide enough to test the craftsmanship of the hinges. "What is it this time?" he bellowed, knowing his father would be just inside, waiting for him.

At just under six feet tall and with the look of a hardened warrior, most men would have cowered to be the object of his frustration. His father simply ignored his belligerence. One sentence escaped his lips, the very words Ronan feared most.

"Your bride will be arriving next month," his father declared from the center of the great hall.

"My *what?*" Ronan could hardly get the words out fast enough.

"You heard me," his father answered sharply.

"I have not agreed to marry anyone yet," Ronan said. "I should not have a bride arriving, only a woman."

"You're old enough to have had at least two bairns by now," his father said.

"I'm not getting married," Ronan growled. "And certainly not to some stranger of a woman you chose on a whim."

"You'll meet her when she visits. Next month. And then, provided she is as suitable as she seems, you will offer for her," Laird Murdoch instructed calmly.

"I'm not getting married," Ronan repeated vehemently. He grew weary of this constant battle.

A knock sounded on the door, and Brother Gilbert slipped quietly inside.

"Apologies, my lords. I have need to speak with the laird," he explained.

"Come in, Gilbert, you're not interrupting anything," Laird Murdoch said, gesturing him toward the warm fire.

"I wanted to be certain you sent that request in, laird. I won't be here much longer and I'll need time to train the new man," Brother Gilbert said.

"Where are you going?" Ronan asked, taken aback. This was the first he had heard of Brother Gilbert leaving. The old monk had lived at Calder Keep for all of Ronan's twenty-five years. He'd be sorely missed.

"I've been recalled to Dornoch Cell in the northeast," Brother Gilbert explained sadly, "I found out a month ago, but I hadn't the heart to tell you yet."

Ronan couldn't find the words to answer Brother Gilbert's shocking statement.

"Aye, Gilbert, I sent the message. The lad who took the invitation to Lady Sybilla continued south to Oxford. We'll have us a scholar in short order, I imagine," Laird Murdoch replied.

"He went *where?*" Ronan asked. Why did it feel like he was the only reasonable person in this room?

"Well he went first to Derbyshire to deliver Lady Sybilla's invitation to visit, and right about now he ought to be arriving at Oxford to request a scholar to replace our Brother Gilbert," his father answered.

"You invited not one, but *two* English nobles to come into the Highlands and make permanent residence?" Ronan couldn't contain his exasperation. "There's no way in heaven or hell I'm marrying anyone, but most certainly not an Englishwoman."

"Ronan, we've spoken of this many times. An alliance with the English nobility will help us move the cattle south. We need a more efficient route, and we need friends in high places to get it. Marriage is a good start, and having a scholar knowledgeable on such matters will only help our reputation and efforts," Laird Murdoch said with annoyance.

"Father, we are at war with the English. Our king invaded England last winter, or have you forgotten?" Ronan retorted.

"He also married an Englishwoman himself," Brother Gilbert added.

"Oh, not you, too," Ronan turned around to glare properly at Gilbert.

"I counseled your father to do just as he's done," Brother Gilbert replied, "One can never have too many allies, particularly in times of war."

"Allies who will stab you in the back at the first opportunity," Ronan muttered, his mood blackening by the minute. "I've heard enough. I'll take my leave."

Ronan stalked back out of the keep, praying for the rain. At least then something would feel right – the weather would match his thoughts. He heard footsteps rushing behind him as he cut across the courtyard. Turning to look, he discovered that Brother Gilbert was nearly upon him.

"Ronan, I know I should've mentioned it sooner," Brother Gilbert said, folding his hands beneath his robes as he walked.

Ronan ran a hand through his shoulder-length dark hair. "How much longer will we have you?" Ronan asked, frowning at his friend. The man who replaced him had better be good, or Ronan would be giving him hell.

"Only two or three months, I'm afraid," Brother Gilbert answered, "I'll be gone by Yule."

"Did you really tell my father to marry me to an Englishwoman?" Ronan had to know Gilbert's thoughts on the matter. He couldn't believe anyone would think that a good idea.

Brother Gilbert smiled weakly. "You have to marry someone," he said, "It might as well be someone who will benefit Clan Calder."

Ronan stopped walking. "You cannot mean that," he asserted.

Brother Gilbert stopped as well, and looked right into Ronan's hazel eyes.

Sent as a young man to advise Laird Murdoch's father, Brother Gilbert had always been a part of Ronan's life. When Ronan was a boy, Brother Gilbert had been of middling age. Always fit and never sickly, Ronan had never thought of him as an old man. Looking at him now, he began to notice what he hadn't before. Silver hair had overtaken all but the last strands of brown. He was still fit, but he was slowing down. There was a heaviness in his step where once he had climbed mountains and forded rivers with ease. Perhaps retiring to his brotherhood of monks wasn't a bad thing. Ronan still didn't have to be happy about it.

At length, Brother Gilbert spoke again. The serious look in his eyes told Ronan it wouldn't be something he wanted to hear.

"Don't live your life in fear of the past or the future, Ronan," he said. "Not every woman dies in childbirth. There is a good chance your wife will be fine."

"There is just as good a chance she and the bairn would both be dead a year from now," Ronan replied. "Clan Calder is cursed. I won't risk the life of another woman simply to further my father's ambition."

"There's no curse," Brother Gilbert chided him. His tone hinted at just how many times he'd said such a thing over the years. "There is a plan that we cannot see, but there is no curse."

Ronan waved a hand dismissively at the monk. He was forever finding ways to proselytize. Somehow it was both his greatest flaw and his greatest strength.

"Women die everywhere in childbirth," Ronan said, "But more of them die here than in any of the other clans. Why? Why is that? Until we can fix it, I won't be subjecting a woman to it."

"Even an Englishwoman?" Brother Gilbert pressed.

"I won't be taking an Englishwoman to bed, so it won't matter," Ronan retorted.

"Good luck telling your father that," Brother Gilbert said, with a chuckle.

Brother Gilbert took his leave as Ronan approached the stables. Sólas stomped his hooves impatiently as Ronan began re-saddling him. The horse's hot breath rose in wisps through the crisp September air. Ronan gave him a gentle rub to calm him down while he fastened the last straps into place. Sólas was ever restless this time of the year, as though he knew he'd be cooped up in the coming months.

As he rode, he considered how he might manage this new turn of events. He was not going to marry the Englishwoman, so he needed to decide now how he would be getting out of it. He could find a suitable Scotswoman, but then he would still be putting an innocent woman at risk of untimely death. He quickly discounted that option.

He could completely ignore the woman, but then he ran the risk of insulting her and heightening tensions even further with the English. No, that wouldn't do either.

A particularly icy blast swept over the hills, giving Ronan a feeling of foreboding. He wasn't certain what to do about the impending Englishwoman, but he knew he must do something. The winter was fast approaching, Brother Gilbert was leaving, and his father had invited two English visitors to Calder Keep. Change was in the air, and judging by the chill it wouldn't be for the better.

Chapter Three

September 24, 1136

Adelina's hands trembled as she approached Master Gregory's cottage. It was a tidy, well-appointed home made of thatch and timbers, two stories tall and just as wide. A sweet-smelling rose bush, decorated by dozens of small, deep pink blooms, greeted visitors at the front door.

"Now don't forget, love, I'm here if you need me," her father said quietly.

Adelina smiled at him. "I know, papa," she assured him. They had always been of a mind, Adelina and her father. She knew his thoughts without him ever needing to voice them. And she knew with certainty that he would always be there if she needed him.

She took a long, shuddering breath before knocking on the door. Her father gave her shoulder a supportive squeeze while they awaited an answer. He had worn his finest clothes and, given the amount of coin he spent on fabric, that was saying quite a lot. He was a full head taller than her, and he grew rounder in the middle with each passing winter. His blue eyes were a match for her brother's, a shade darker than Adelina's own.

A tall, lithe woman of middling age opened the door. Her gray-brown hair was loosely braided over her shoulder.

"Come in, come in," she urged, gesturing them into the house. "They're waiting for you in the hall."

Around a corner and down three steps, the woman opened a smaller door, revealing three men seated at a trestle table in the middle of a long, narrow hall. They had been deep in conversation until Adelina and her father entered the room. A telling silence greeted them. Adelina's heart raced. Would they let her in?

The man on her left stood. What little bit of hair remained to him was fading quickly from brown to silver. He smiled warmly at her, easing her nerves just enough to bring her further into the room.

"Master Henry, Mistress Adelina," he said, acknowledging them, "Thank you for coming. I am Master Gregory, and this is Master Thomas and Master Adam. Please, be seated.

"Mistress Adelina," he continued, looking directly at her with piercing green eyes, "You have applied not once, not twice, but three times to attend lectures with your brother at Oxford. Such efforts show great strength of spirit, conviction, and tenacity. We know you also to be a commendable intellectual, if your brother's praises are to be taken into consideration. Armed with this knowledge of your character and talents, we have a proposition for you.

"You wish to be a student of Oxford, and we require aid with a delicate matter. Perhaps, we might be able to assist one another."

Master Gregory paused, as though searching for the best phrasing of his request. Adelina was not inclined to wait patiently. Instead, she made her own assessment.

"So, in exchange for my help with your 'delicate matter' you will allow me to attend lectures at Oxford?"

"Mistress Adelina, we would never be permitted to accept a woman, especially a common-born woman, no matter her family's wealth, at Oxford. We could, however, allow you to sit in on an assortment of lectures for a smaller fee than that of a student," Master Adam, a younger man with a scruffy brown beard explained.

"That alone is a privilege we have yet to bestow upon any of the fairer sex. That we are now considering it is no small accomplishment on your part," Master Thomas added with a supportive smile.

"Surely other educated women have made similar requests in the past," Adelina remarked. She knew that no other women had been admitted, but she refused to believe it was simply that no women had tried.

"None with your aptitude for the subjects covered by our lectures," Master Gregory said finally. "Which is why we believe you might be the solution to our problem. Laird Murdoch Calder has requested that we send him a scholar to replace a clergyman he is losing."

Adelina's mind raced, gathering all the implications of that statement. She was glad to be sitting down already, else she may have embarrassed herself with unsteadiness. Surely Master Gregory would clarify just exactly what he meant by that. Before long Adelina realized that she would be left wondering.

"Master Gregory," she began as calmly as she could, "Forgive me if I misunderstand. Are you implying that you would like to send *me* to Laird Calder?"

"As we are at war with Scotland, we did not think it prudent for us to send one of England's most promising scholars from our most prestigious school to advise the enemy," Master Adam said, as though that was an acceptable answer.

Adelina stood at his insult. She knew better. "So am I to understand that you believe me too stupid to give the laird good advice? Why even consider admitting me for lectures, then?"

"Mistress Adelina, please forgive Master Adam's poor choice of words," Master Gregory soothed, "What he was trying to say is that we would like to level it as a test, a challenge if you will."

"And how do you propose to measure my success or failure at such a test?" Adelina could feel the heat in her cheeks. She had expected an interesting meeting. She had even been prepared to withstand a few minor insults if it meant they'd tolerate her presence in the lectures. But sending her to Scotland, during a war, for a position they believed beyond her was something else altogether. At the very least, she knew some sort of trick was afoot. What exactly that might be, she had yet to determine.

"We will correspond with Laird Calder in six months to inquire as to your usefulness to him. Should you prove an asset to his clan, we will ask him to allow you to leave periodically and take one of our courses to further your education," Master Thomas replied.

Adelina paced, considering the offer. The men waited in silence, watching her. If she accepted, it sounded as though she'd be living in the Highlands for the foreseeable future. Away from her family, away from her friends, in the heart of enemy territory. Probably there was some other factor she hadn't considered yet as well, but truth be told she was still reeling from the ridiculousness of their proposition. And, most importantly, she certainly wouldn't be attending lectures in the way she had envisioned.

On the other hand, that they made her an offer of attendance at all, even so meager as this one, was nothing short of a miracle. A woman like Adelina, of common birth, ought to be grateful for the opportunity. She could prove her own worth and begin a formal education like no woman had done before her. Many of the men who attended Oxford did so in the hopes of landing a position such as the one offered to her now.

Master Gregory cleared his throat. Adelina turned to regard him as her mind continued to weigh her options.

"Do you not wish to consult your father on this matter?" Master Gregory asked, as though he were delivering some great bit of advice.

She did want to know her father's opinion, but they had decided beforehand that in order to show her strength and independence, she would conduct all business unless absolutely necessary. Honestly, given what Adelina knew of her father, it was nothing short of miraculous that he hadn't said anything yet. He surely had thoughts on sending his only daughter on what would be at least a month's ride into Scotland, by her estimation.

"My daughter will make her own decision on the matter," her father answered brusquely. "However, I have several questions for my own edification."

"Of course, Master Henry, ask as you please," Master Gregory responded, gesturing widely with his hands.

"How far into the Highlands is this Laird Calder's holding?" her father asked. Adelina had wondered the same thing herself.

"'Tis twenty days' walk, ten days by cart with two horses," Master Thomas said.

"And who will be accompanying Adelina on this adventure?" her father continued his interrogation.

"There is a caravan of merchants leaving for the north in a few days' time. They have agreed to escort our scholar safely to Inverness for a fee. From there, it is a few hours' walk or ride due east into Calder lands," Master Gregory answered.

"So 'twill be twenty days, then," Adelina said, her mind calculating. "Fifty men, some with their wives, and all with their wares will be traveling slowly. Horses and carts won't make a difference if they're laden with goods and passengers."

"With rest stops and a large group, aye, twenty days seems likely," Master Thomas agreed.

Adelina looked to her father. She didn't want his approval; she knew she didn't need it. The decision was hers. He looked her in the eyes and gave her a soft half-smile. Sadness crept into his gaze. Adelina understood, then, that before she herself realized it, he knew what her answer would be. She smiled back at him. Few fathers would be so supportive.

"What say you, Mistress Adelina? Will you do us this service in exchange for your schooling?" Master Gregory's voice carefully masked impatience, or attempted to do so. Everyone else had been happy to let her spend a few moments contemplating a decision that would affect the rest of her life and that of her family.

Turning to face Master Gregory, Adelina pulled her shoulders back and stood straight. She stared him down for several seconds, undaunted by the decision before her.

She took a deep breath, then asked, "When do I leave?"

Chapter Four

October 17, 1136

Raindrops struck Adelina's dripping skin as she halted her mare in the courtyard at Calder Keep. The rain fell so forcefully in the wind that it looked like sheets being aired after a wash. Everything Adelina owned was drenched. She could hardly see her surroundings amidst the downpour, let alone find the stables. Dismounting into a puddle of muddy water, she wandered off to the left side of the towering gray keep she had managed to spot across from her.

"Can I help you?" A man's voice shouted at her over the cacophony of rain. Between the noise of the weather and his heavy brogue, Adelina hardly understood what he had said.

"The stables?" She shouted her question.

The man pointed in the direction she had been headed, gesturing that it was back a ways further. Adelina sighed, leading her mare toward the first building she saw.

A wooden structure with a sharp peak, covered in thatch, the stables felt like heaven compared with the rain whipping outside. Adelina patted her horse. She had affectionately named the creature Phaeton after one of the immortal horses who pulled the chariot of the goddess of the dawn, according to ancient Greek beliefs. It mattered not that 'twas a man's name. Adelina thought it beautiful and wished her fine steed nothing but a long life of sunny mornings.

Toward the back of the stables, Adelina found Phaeton an empty stall. A figure in the adjoining stall startled her as she walked past. She gasped in surprise at the unexpected company.

"Hello, milady. Sorry to give you a fright," said a man as he stepped toward her out of the stall. He had been brushing his horse, and Adelina could now see that he wore a long black robe. He was an older man, old enough to be her grandfather, and had a kindly look to his dark brown eyes. "Can I help you with anything?" he asked, "I don't believe I've seen you here before."

"Thank you, Brother –" Adelina paused, giving the man an opportunity to supply his name. She knew him to be a Benedictine monk from his robes.

"Gilbert," he finished for her. "I am Brother Gilbert."

"I am Adelina, daughter of Henry Matheson, of Oxford," she said, bowing politely as she introduced herself.

Brother Gilbert blanched. "Oxford, you say?" he asked, wringing his hands. "That can't be right."

"I beg your pardon?" Adelina wasn't certain she'd heard him correctly. "Is there something wrong?"

Brother Gilbert looked around the stables, then helped Adelina get Phaeton settled in her stall while he continued the conversation.

"What brings you to Calder all the way from Oxford?" he queried, apparently ignoring her question.

"I was asked to come here," she replied, pulling herself up a little straighter. "Master Gregory met with me in person, wanting me to come to Calder and replace the scholar who is leaving."

Brother Gilbert's jaw dropped at that statement. It took him several moments to collect both his thoughts and his decorum. Adelina didn't give him time to respond. His reaction said it all.

"Brother Gilbert," she began sternly, "I did not travel overland for twenty-one days through mountains and rain only to be turned away. I will be staying here and acting as scholar, as was requested by Laird Calder."

He started to speak, but Adelina held up her hand to silence him.

"I can tell from your reaction that some sort of misunderstanding has occurred, but I have the paperwork to prove my claim, assuming it survived that horrendous downpour. Now, if you don't mind, could you point me in the direction of the current scholar serving Laird Calder?"

A belly-deep, hand-on-your-knee laugh was his only answer for several minutes. Adelina was growing impatient, and she became more and more concerned that she was the center of some sort of jest. When she put her hands to her hips, Brother Gilbert finally got a hold of himself.

"Adelina, you and I have many things to discuss. Why don't you join me in the library so that we can speak privately for a time? I believe it's important that we do so before you meet the laird," he explained.

"Will you be telling me what was so amusing to you?" Adelina asked tartly as she headed for the door.

"I thought you knew I was Laird Calder's resident scholar during our entire conversation. That you didn't took me by surprise," he replied.

"Oh!" Adelina exclaimed, "Well, why didn't you just say so! What a miracle that I happened upon you."

"More than I think you know, lass," Brother Gilbert said more soberly.

"How do you mean?" Adelina wondered aloud.

Brother Gilbert gave her a sympathetic look but didn't answer her question. Instead, he led her further away from the courtyard, behind the stables, past the smithy and the chapel, to the small library. To have a library at all was something of a feat, and for such a small holding to possess one so great was remarkable.

The building was square, and like all the others it was made of wooden timbers with a thatched roof. Inside, Adelina was met with the familiar smell of parchment and vellum. To her left, on the same wall as the doorway, a long table with two chairs rested beneath the only window in sight. Three tall shelves ran parallel to the table across the entire length of the building. They were filled with books, scrolls, and loose sheets of parchment waiting for binding. The opposite corner of the building, and the walls across from her, were hidden behind the massive shelves.

"I will certainly miss it," Brother Gilbert said sadly.

"Surely your monastery has a library to rival even this one," Adelina observed encouragingly.

Brother Gilbert smiled. "The monastery does, yes. But the priory has a much smaller collection, and with a far smaller scope of subject matter. This is truly a fine collection of manuscripts," he sighed. "No matter, we must attend to the business at hand."

Adelina wandered over to the nearest shelf to peruse its contents while she listened to Brother Gilbert. She looked at him periodically and smiled to ensure he knew he still held her attention. Or at least most of it.

"Did Master Gregory say why they chose you to fill Laird Calder's request for a scholar?" he asked, linking his hands behind his back.

Adelina thought for a moment before answering. She could hardly say that they thought her so dumb she couldn't be a threat, even as a counselor to the enemy. Whatever the reason, she didn't want to give anyone reason to doubt her ability to do the job.

"He never gave what I would call a satisfactory explanation," she said finally, "They were reluctant to let any of their current students leave in the middle of their studies."

"I see," he replied. Adelina felt that he did, in fact, see. Perhaps he even saw too much. "Now I ask you, as someone qualified for the position of scholar, why would the great men at Oxford choose you, of all the people available, to come here with us?"

Brother Gilbert leveled the question without judgment. Adelina could tell from his tone that he was attempting to instruct her. Seeing as it was a good opportunity to prove her merit, Adelina played along.

"Advising a Highland laird, particularly while England is at war with Scotland, is not an exceptionally glamorous post," Adelina answered. "Many of the students wouldn't have accepted it, either for its dangers or for its lack of prestige. No offense, Brother," she added quickly.

Brother Gilbert smiled. "I, too, was assigned to this post. I certainly didn't choose it," he conceded. "So we have now some understanding of why the other students wouldn't be chosen. But that doesn't explain why they chose *you*."

"They knew I would do it," Adelina admitted defeatedly. "They knew I would do anything to be able to attend their lectures."

"Surely, you're not the only would-be student desperate to prove their worth," he said kindly. "So then we must ask, how are you different from every other student at Oxford?"

Adelina thought for a moment. She wasn't any worse of a student, or poorer than everyone. She wasn't the only applicant of common birth, though that was rarer. And then it struck her. She felt the realization like a punch to her gut.

"I'm a woman," she said in shock, "They sent me because I'm a woman."

Brother Gilbert nodded, and pulled out a chair at the long table. Adelina sat, still reeling from her new understanding of the situation. They hadn't sent her to test her abilities. They had sent her as an insult to the laird. How could she not have seen this? Perhaps she wasn't ready to be a scholar after all.

"I see the thoughts flickering across your face, lass, and you listen well," Brother Gilbert said sternly. "Do not beat yourself down. Everyone else is going to do that for you. You are here to prove to them that, woman or no, you are the scholar of Calder Keep."

Chapter Five

Ronan drank in the soft, earthy smell that followed the rain. He carefully sidestepped the mud puddles that had filled in ruts around the courtyard. Typically, Ronan relished the rains as they came through the Highlands. He enjoyed the cool, misty calm they left in their wake. This afternoon, though, he was riled again. Which made it difficult to enjoy the beautiful weather.

His father had sent him to get Brother Gilbert so that they might have a meeting. About what, the tight-lipped laird wouldn't say, which perturbed Ronan to no end. He would be laird himself one day, and he needed to be privy to the decisions made while overseeing clan affairs. He, of course, reminded his father of this, to no avail. The laird's silence meant that the matter had to do with Ronan himself, which was even more concerning. Probably something about the unlucky lass his father had invited, from *England*, to come and stay.

Ronan reached the door to the library, where one could almost always find Brother Gilbert face-first in some dusty tome. On top of all of it – the potential betrothal, the secret meeting his father was arranging – Ronan was quite possibly the most upset at being sent to fetch Brother Gilbert like a simple errand boy. He had also been certain to remind his father that there were *actual* errand boys to do just such a task, once more to no avail.

He angrily threw open the door to the library, eliciting a jump and a gasp from the beautiful young woman standing just inside. Her fiery red hair caught the light that flooded in from the doorway. She nearly dropped the parchment in her hands.

"You're not Brother Gilbert," he said.

"I should think not," she replied, giving his intrusion her full attention. "He'll be just a minute, I believe. If you're desperate I could always attempt to fill in."

"Unfortunately, I believe only Brother Gilbert will do in this instance," Ronan replied. He couldn't help but smile in amusement at her jest.

She walked over to Brother Gilbert's study table and sat in his chair, facing Ronan. She folded her hands demurely on the table and stared him down as she said, "I insist."

"Very well," he conceded, sitting down opposite her to match. "Laird Calder has asked Brother Gilbert to join him in the hall."

"Oh, dear," she said, feigning seriousness, "I do believe you'll need Brother Gilbert for that."

Ronan guessed that she must be the noble bride his father had invited. She spoke and dressed like a well-to-do Englishwoman, though it was curious that she had somehow ended up in the library instead of the keep. He had been determined not to like her at all, in order to make his rejection of her easier, but her playfulness was charming away his foul mood. He still wouldn't be marrying her, but he supposed he could at least attempt a conversation.

"It just so happens I have another query for the good man. Mayhap you could help me with that one?" Ronan had no idea where that had come from. He didn't have anything else to ask Brother Gilbert, and he hadn't the faintest idea what he could ask the entrancing young lady across the table from him. All he knew was that he desperately wanted to continue this conversation.

"Very well, try me," she challenged.

Ronan's eyes strayed once more to the deep red color of her hair, fashioned into a long braid that began at her forehead and ran down to the small of her back. "I have heard rumors that women who have red hair also possess magical powers," he said, hoping he didn't sound as foolish as he felt, "Do you think it true?"

She laughed at him, yet it somehow made him feel better instead of worse.

"My father always said red hair gives you protection from the Devil himself," she replied, "So I suppose in a way, that's sort of like magic."

"Is your father a wise man?" Ronan asked.

"I like to think so," she answered without hesitation. A smile formed on her rose-colored lips, and Ronan found his eyes wandering to places they ought not. For an Englishwoman, she certainly was a pretty lass. And witty, too, as he judged thus far.

"Why are you smiling, lass?" he queried.

"You were going to ask Brother Gilbert about the magical qualities of red hair?" She had to press her lips together to contain a giggle. Ronan rather wished she hadn't. He would like to hear her laugh. Indeed, he couldn't help but smile at his own foolishness.

"Aye, lass, you've caught me," he conceded. "Mayhap I was in no hurry to part company with a beautiful lady." What on earth was he saying? The words rolled right out with a will of their own, 'twould seem.

A blush the color of wild raspberries flooded her cheeks, but instead of looking away like most lasses, she met his gaze dead-on. Her blue eyes were the color of a clear summer sky, not a cloud in sight. Lord help him, he hoped Brother Gilbert never returned.

"Right," he began, grateful that she chose to ignore his embarrassing statement, "Let's try something of substance. What were you studying so carefully when I opened the door?"

"*Opened?*" she countered, raising a delicate eyebrow, the same hue as her vermilion hair.

Ronan cleared his throat. "Shoved?" he offered. Maybe he had been a bit rough with the door.

"Hurled," she stated, "You hurled that door open."

"So you admit that I opened it," he said with a grin.

She waved a hand dismissively, "'Tis semantics," she replied.

"Only because you lost," he retorted, folding his arms and relaxing back into his chair. "Now what were you reading when I so brutishly interrupted you?"

"St. Augustine," she said, lifting the parchment off the table to peruse it once more.

"And what does he have to say?"

"'In doing what we ought, we deserve no praise, for it is our duty,'" she read aloud.

"Yes, I've never much cared for Augustine," Ronan said, "I don't think he and I are of a mind."

She managed to look down her nose at him, while seated and shorter of stature. She did not, however look surprised by his outrageous statement about one of the greatest theologians ever born. Probably not a good sign, that.

"He also says, 'Love is the beauty of the soul,'" she offered, as though that helped.

Ronan shook his head, "Wrong again, Saint Augustine," he said vehemently.

"You cannot possibly disagree with that!" she exclaimed, "It's the simplest, truest statement he makes."

"You chose that line because you thought I would agree with it?" Ronan asked. Lord help him, he was much more interested in the thoughts of this enchanting lady than of St. Augustine. Brother Gilbert had drilled every line of every theological work ever written into him while he was yet a lad. He knew well the words of which she spoke. He also knew he should leave and find Brother Gilbert. Already he was dallying too long with a lass he had no business courting. Hadn't he made up his mind to avoid the woman his father was forcing upon him?

"I thought a man so given to flattery may be familiar with the topic of love," she answered, sounding entirely too certain of herself.

"I'll have you know, lass, that I have never before given a lady such a compliment as I gave to you," Ronan responded with as much sincerity as he could. He wanted her to know the truth of it, not think him some sort of runaround. Though really, he shouldn't care either way.

She blushed once more, and he had to clasp his hands to stop from touching her cheek to feel its heat.

"Ronan!" Brother Gilbert's surprised voice sounded from the doorway. "I didn't expect to find you here. I see you've met Adelina."

Adelina. The name was as beautiful as the maiden. Ronan knew he wouldn't soon forget it.

"She was just instructing me on Augustine," Ronan explained to Brother Gilbert, smiling wryly at Adelina.

"Good, it needs doing," Brother Gilbert retorted, "You're sure to have forgotten my lessons by now, whether in word or in deed I dare not guess. What business brings you?"

"Father wants to see you," Ronan said, rising to leave with Brother Gilbert, "He'll be unhappy at having waited so long already. Lady Adelina," he turned to face her, taking her hand and pressing it to his lips, "It has been my pleasure."

As much as Ronan wanted to be furious at his father for thrusting a marriage upon him, he had to admit that there was a possibility he could enjoy the company of Lady Adelina.

Chapter Six

Lady Adelina. He had called her *Lady* Adelina. Lord, he thought she was a noblewoman. She hadn't even had enough time to stop reeling from the realization that he was the laird's son before he went and called her *lady*. And she certainly hadn't had enough time to set him straight. He shot out of the door before she could manage a sound.

Once she wrapped her mind around all of this new information, Adelina thought over the rest of his visit. He was damned handsome, that was for sure. When he had thrown open the door he had scared her half to death, then she turned to see a giant of a man filling the modest doorway. He was built of solid muscle, and he had the most expressive eyes she had ever seen. Every thought flitted across his face, every emotion seemed to spend just the briefest moment there in the open. She didn't know him well enough yet to tell what each subtle change had meant, but in time she would.

Though she greatly admired his physique, Adelina enjoyed his company all the more. When he had first entered and insisted that only Brother Gilbert could help him, she had taken insult. It soon became clear, however, that he only meant well. By the end of it he had been quite charming.

In the midst of her meditation on Ronan's fine qualities, the door creaked open once more. Brother Gilbert's silvery head appeared, followed quickly by the rest of him. More time must have passed than she had realized, or his trip to the keep was brief indeed. He walked over to the table and sat down across from her, where Ronan had been, grabbing a tome off the shelf along the way.

"What's that one?" Adelina asked, unable to contain her curiosity. She was hoping to spend a sizeable portion of her first months here scouring the treasures within the keep's library.

"Donatus," Brother Gilbert replied, opening the book on the table between them, "*Ars minor.*"

"*The Smaller Art*," Adelina translated happily. She had read it many times in her study of Latin. It was the foremost text for teaching the language to students.

"So you do know Latin at least," he mumbled.

Of course she knew Latin. What a ridiculous revelation. "How could I be a scholar without it?" she asked, taken aback.

"And you can write it as well? The Calder laird is a fine thinker and has a firm grasp on the language, but he still requires assistance with composition," he explained.

"Brother Gilbert, please. I assure you I am perfectly able to handle any use of the language," Adelina said with exasperation.

"Mmm," was all he added by way of a reply. Adelina watched him carefully leaf through pages. He was clearly heading toward conditional statements to quiz her. A protest caught in her throat when her eyes shifted from the pages of the book to Brother Gilbert's hands. Red, cracked, dry, and nearly bleeding, Adelina knew immediately that they must be terribly painful. Dry hands were a common complaint around the industrious students and masters at Oxford. One of the first lessons

Gemma taught Adelina was a tried and true remedy for just such an ailment.

"Brother Gilbert," Adelina said gently, "If you might indulge me, I would like to help your hands."

Brother Gilbert looked down at them, but then shrugged. "They've been this way for years, lass," he replied, "I've tried all manner of curatives, but nothing seems to help."

"Regardless," Adelina pressed, getting to her feet to fetch her satchel from the nearby pile of her belongings, "I insist. I believe I have just the thing."

The look of skepticism never left Brother Gilbert's face, but he did finally humor her. Adelina carefully set her satchel on the table next to Donatus' famous text. She opened it slowly, ensuring the many jars, some even made of glass, remained intact and full of their precious ingredients. Brother Gilbert's eyes widened.

"Where did you get that?" he asked, his voice full of awe and tinged with suspicion.

"My father had the satchel specially made to carry jars and bottles without spilling. My dearest friend taught me what to fill them with," Adelina answered proudly.

She pulled out a large glass bottle, a linen cloth, and a jar of salve. After unstoppering the bottle, she carefully poured some of the thin brown liquid onto the cloth to apply it to Brother Gilbert's aching hands.

"That smells better than it looks," he observed, eyeing the bottle.

Adelina grinned. The look of it always put people off. "A decoction of willow bark," she explained, "It should help to cleanse the open wounds and relieve some of the pain."

Brother Gilbert watched intently as Adelina applied the decoction. When she had finished, he slowly wiggled his fingers. He let out a deep sigh, as though the weight of the world no longer rested on his poor, cracked hands.

"That already has helped," he said, as though he hardly believed his own statement.

"'Tis only temporary," Adelina warned him, "You'll need to apply it two to three times each day for several weeks to allow your hands to heal fully."

He glanced at her satchel, his eyes calculating. "Have you enough of it for that?"

Adelina shook her head. "Nay, I didn't bring much. Just enough for emergencies. I can easily make more, if someone can point me toward a willow tree."

"There's one nearby, next to the loch," Brother Gilbert offered, "I'll show you myself tomorrow." He was nearly grinning now.

She smiled back at him, opening the jar of salve and scooping out a generous pinch. "May I?" she asked, reaching for his hand.

He nodded, extending them out to her. She smoothed the salve into his wounds, ensuring she left a thick coating that wouldn't wear away too quickly. After she finished with his first hand, she heard him inhale deeply.

"Rose?" he queried, inhaling one more time. "And," he began, thinking.

"Mallow," Adelina supplied. "Both soothe and heal the skin."

Brother Gilbert nodded, apparently satisfied by her explanation. There was silence as Adelina finished applying the salve to his other hand and carefully packed up her satchel, wiping her hands clean in the process. She put Donatus back on the shelf to spare Brother Gilbert the trouble of handling the hefty tome whilst covered in salve. He looked a long moment at the book as she lifted it away.

"He thought you were a noblewoman," Brother Gilbert said into the silence.

"I beg your pardon?" Adelina asked, returning to her seat. She knew where this conversation was headed. Yet, for no good reason, she desperately hoped she was wrong.

"Lass, I like you. You'll do a fine job as a scholar, and apparently as a healer as well," Brother Gilbert explained gently, "But you and I both know that Ronan, as the laird's son, must marry a woman of equal status."

"Brother Gilbert," Adelina said, narrowing her eyes, "why exactly are you reminding me of something we both already know?"

"Consider it a favor in kind, even if unsolicited," he replied, "We've had many a noblewoman come to call, and not a one has he treated with such regard as I saw he had for you today. Even once he learns that you are not what he believes, be on your guard. He may pursue you, but he cannot and would not marry you. 'Twould be a hard lesson to learn, and one I wouldn't wish upon anyone. Particularly a lovely lass such as yourself."

"Are you suggesting that I am going to fall flat on my face for his flowery words?" Adelina bristled, "I would never be so stupid."

"Nevertheless," Brother Gilbert continued, "I feel it is my responsibility to mention. And now," he said, rising from his chair, "It is time for the most unpleasant task before us today."

Adelina stood, raising an eyebrow in question.

"We must present Laird Calder with his new scholar," he explained, "I don't imagine he'll take the insult from your Oxford masters gracefully. God help you, lass."

Brother Gilbert graciously gave Adelina a short time in which to see to her appearance after a long day of traveling through the rain. Her hair had taken more of a beating than she realized, and she was left with no choice but to re-braid it entirely. With a sigh of resignation, she began the tedious process of imposing order, strand by unruly strand. Unfortunately, this also gave her time to ruminate.

Of course she wasn't suited to be the wife of a laird. Such a ridiculous notion had never even entered her thoughts. And yet, Brother Gilbert's quick dismissal of her had stung. Why? Why was she being so foolish? What made her feel the loss of something she never wanted to begin with? All her life, Adelina knew she was destined for a mediocre marriage at best. If, by some miracle, a baron had needed her father's money desperately enough to marry for it, she would have been grudgingly accepted into the echelons of nobility.

No, Adelina had no delusional aspirations of a grand marriage to some lord, or laird, as the case may be. She was going to prove herself a capable scholar and an intelligent woman. She was going to be the first woman to take courses at Oxford, and she was going to do everything in her power to afford other women the same opportunity. But Adelina Matheson was absolutely, under no circumstances, going to fall in love with some charming laird's son.

Chapter Seven

Ronan's curiosity was piqued, though he'd be hard-pressed to admit such a thing to anyone. Lady Adelina had been on his mind since he crossed paths with her several hours ago. He had noticed, however, that his father hadn't mentioned her or called Ronan to meet with her or her family. Perhaps Laird Calder was unaware of her arrival. Ronan decided to bring this to his father's attention, and then seek out Lady Adelina for a short walk through the grounds before supper. He still had absolutely no intention of marrying the poor lass, but he might be persuaded to speak with her again, if only to help her settle into her stay.

Laird Calder was a rough man, in every sense of the phrase. Ronan had learned long ago that his father was not to be troubled with trivial matters like sorrow or guilt. After his mother had died birthing his youngest brother, who had also been lost that day, Ronan had his elder sister to comfort him in his grief. He had been ten years old that day. But when his sister, Maggie, also succumbed to her laboring eight years later, Ronan had no one. His father wouldn't hear a single word of it, wouldn't even allow their names to be uttered.

Beatrix, his now seven-year-old niece, lived with her father's family. Only Ronan corresponded with them to inquire after her. Only Ronan remembered to send her a gift and a letter on her birthday. Maggie had hoped that by naming her daughter "blessed," Beatrix might avoid the same fate as all the other women in their family. Ronan prayed every day that his niece could live the long, happy life every mother deserved. He didn't know what her future would bring, but he did know that losing another woman in childbirth would destroy him. Which is exactly why he could never, *ever* marry. He simply couldn't risk putting a woman he loved through such torture.

Shaking his head to rid himself of his dark thoughts, Ronan climbed the front steps of the keep. Before he could grab a handle, the large oaken doors into the hall swung open toward him. Recovering quickly, Ronan managed to catch the nearest one and step to the side. Two elegant ladies and a well-appointed man walked past him on their way out of the great hall, his father close behind.

"Ah, just in time!" Laird Calder said cheerfully when he caught sight of his son.

"Ronan, this is Lady Sybilla Blakewell, and her father Lord John Blakewell. My lord and lady, this is my son, Ronan."

"A pleasure to meet you, my lord," Lady Sybilla greeted him in a silvery voice. She had blonde hair the color of wheat at the harvest, golden and glimmering. Her porcelain white skin told Ronan that she had spent hardly a day out of doors, even during her journey to Calder Keep. She had brown eyes, flecked with gold to match her hair. Her tall, delicate frame was clothed in a pale pink gown. She looked every inch a lady. The other woman, who appeared of an age with Lady Sybilla, was clearly her handmaid. She bowed alongside her mistress.

Ronan was speechless. Who was this woman? He had just met the lady his father had brought from England to convince him to wed, hadn't he? And then Ronan remembered. His father had said that his messenger was visiting Lady Sybilla. Which would mean that this was the English woman his father wanted him to marry. Then who was Lady Adelina?

Laird Calder cleared his throat, giving Ronan a furious look for being so rude as to ignore the lady's greeting.

"The pleasure is all mine, my lady," Ronan said tersely, unable to pull away from his own thoughts.

"You must be tired from your long journey," Laird Calder declared quickly, doing his best to smooth over Ronan's blunder. "We look forward to your company at supper this evening."

"Of course, Laird," Lady Sybilla replied demurely, averting her gaze respectfully away from his father. "We are grateful for your invitation. I am certain our visit will be – fruitful." She paused for just a breath before her last word, glancing at Ronan out of the corner of her eyes.

Lady Sybilla curtsied gracefully, then descended the steps in a flutter of pink damask. Her maid followed closely on her heels. Her father, Lord Blakewell, had the audacity to wink at Ronan before sauntering on behind his daughter.

Laird Calder turned to him. "Well, you certainly could've been more polite. I ken you don't want a wife, Ronan, but you couldn't even spare a proper greeting for the lass?" He turned back into the keep with an exasperated sigh, disappearing into the hall.

Ronan was right behind him. "Who was that?" he asked, still trying to divine exactly why there were two Englishwomen in his keep.

"God's bones, you heard me! That is your future wife and her father," the laird shouted at him.

"Did you invite more than one potential bride to visit?" Ronan pressed, undaunted by his father's show of anger.

"What are you talking about?" his father was suddenly intent on Ronan's line of questioning. Mayhap he was onto something.

Ronan pushed onward. He had to know what on earth was going on. "If that was Lady Sybilla, then who is the other Englishwoman? Lady Adelina?"

"There are two Englishwomen in my keep?" his father seemed just as concerned as he felt. "Who the hell is Lady Adelina?"

"Ahem."

Ronan and his father turned to find Brother Gilbert standing in the doorway. Lady Adelina was right behind him.

"Laird Calder," Brother Gilbert continued before anyone could say a word, "If you have a moment, there is an important matter which merits discussion."

"What is it?" his father's patience was wearing thin already.

Ronan hoped this discussion wouldn't be too great a trial for Lady Adelina, who was clearly involved in some way.

Brother Gilbert walked into the hall. When Adelina entered after him, the laird looked none too pleased.

"This is an important discussion," he said to her, waving his hand dismissively. "You will be called for if you are needed."

"Laird Calder," Lady Adelina said quietly. Her shoulders tensed as she spoke, "If this is an important meeting, then I must stay as well."

"And who, exactly, are you?" he asked, his eyes narrowing on the poor lass.

"Laird, if I may," Brother Gilbert interjected quickly, standing between the two of them. "This is precisely what I wanted to discuss with you. Now that we're all finished jumping to conclusions, allow me to set the matter straight."

"In as few words as possible, Gilbert," the laird said gruffly.

"Laird Calder, this is Adelina Matheson of Oxford. She is here as my replacement, as we requested," Brother Gilbert explained calmly.

Laird Calder stared at Brother Gilbert for a moment, while the words settled. Once he understood what had happened, he turned his full attention on Adelina.

"Like hell she is!" the laird roared, his face turning redder with each passing moment. "Send her back! How dare they insult me thus! You," he hissed, staring the poor lass down with all his rage, "you are not welcome here."

Chapter Eight

His father stalked down the nearest corridor, growling. Brother Gilbert murmured a hurried apology to Adelina before rushing after the furious laird. The lass stood straight-backed, looking ready to do battle. A fire raged in her pale blue eyes. Her hands were now folded calmly before her as she stood waiting on his beast of a father.

Ronan, for his part, was still reeling from the brief exchange he had just witnessed. He had been flirting with the scholar, not the lady he was meant to marry. Honestly, he almost felt relieved. At least he was still utterly uninterested in his potential bride. When he had believed Adelina to be his betrothed, it had taken him less than an hour to begin worrying over the fact that he was clearly attracted to her. Really, this strange turn of events made everything easier.

Adelina was common-born, which meant that he couldn't marry her. He would be laird one day, and should he ever become weak enough to take a wife, she needed to be able to run his keep and manage portions of the clan's lands. His father's entire aim was to gain favor amongst the English nobility to further his trade interests, something that a marriage to Adelina would certainly not accomplish. Even if it could, his father was clearly unhappy with Adelina's presence, to put it mildly. Which meant that Ronan's illogical attraction to Adelina was entirely harmless. Nothing could come of it, so he had nothing to worry over.

"Is he always so charming?" Adelina asked, breaking the stillness surrounding them. The fire was beginning to leave her eyes now that his father was gone.

"I think it could have gone worse," Ronan replied with a forced smile. He wasn't exactly joking, though. His father tended to have more bark than bite, as folk said. He let his temper get the better of him, but it wasn't often he followed such anger with violent action.

Adelina managed a small smile, but it didn't reach her eyes. She looked away from Ronan, watching the hall where his father had disappeared and furrowing her brow. Any other woman, or man for that matter, would've at least flinched when his father shouted them out of the keep. Most would've left before he finished his sentence.

But not Adelina. She stood there, back straight, head high, and took his anger with hardly a batted lash. Having been on the receiving end of such outbursts many times, Ronan couldn't help but admire her courage. He knew that, whatever she may look on the outside, there was a good chance that she was shaken by the laird's anger at her.

Ronan moved over to Adelina and placed his hand on her delicate shoulder, hoping to show her his support. She gazed up at him over her shoulder, her blue eyes pulling him closer. Ronan's hand suddenly felt hot where it lay on her soft green dress. He leaned closer, his eyes drawn to her neatly rounded lips.

"I should get back to the library," she whispered, freeing herself of his hand, "I need to be familiar with the materials, should the laird require my assistance."

As Ronan watched her walk out of the keep, noticing quite distinctly the enticing sway of her hips as she went, he suddenly realized that this attraction may not be so harmless. He hadn't even known her for a day, and already he was losing control of his thoughts. He would need to be more careful around the charming little scholar. It was no matter. She wouldn't be living inside the keep, since she would stay in the cottage Brother Gilbert was vacating, and in a nearby guest cottage until then. Their paths would rarely cross, except in councils and meetings with his father. 'Twould be easy enough to avoid her.

Having sorted out his thoughts on Adelina, Ronan strode down the hall after his father and Brother Gilbert. Though he realized it would be easier for her to simply disappear, if she had wanted to leave she would already be gone. For some reason, she was choosing to stay, and Ronan respected her for it. Whatever was decided regarding the fate of their new scholar, Ronan wanted to do what he could to help her. "Absolutely not!" the laird's bellowing roar could be heard long before Ronan entered the solar.

"Laird!" Brother Gilbert was shouting right back, bless him. It was one of only a dozen times Ronan could recall the old priest raising his voice. "Hear me out!"

Ronan walked in just as Brother Gilbert made his case on behalf of Adelina.

"I know she is a woman," Brother Gilbert continued, "And I see the insult in sending a woman to you as a scholar."

"Then how could you believe I would allow such mockery! She cannot stay. Her presence only serves to undermine my efforts with England," Laird Calder spat back.

"Should you return her, the masters at Oxford would themselves take insult," Brother Gilbert explained, "Such an affront, especially by a Highlander, would quickly destroy any chances you may have had at peaceable trade in England. It would not take long for word of your offense to reach the ears of the nobility."

The laird was silent a long moment, his hand toying with his thick beard while he considered Brother Gilbert's assessment. Brother

Gilbert never ceased to amaze Ronan with his cunning. The man clearly believed Adelina could do a passing good job as scholar and saw no reason to put her through the humiliation of sending her back. For a brief moment, Ronan believed the old priest had done it. And then his father spoke.

"Should I keep her," he countered through gritted teeth, "they will think me weak, accepting their insult and rolling over like a dog. Any strength they saw in Clan Calder, any fear of our might, would disappear if I allow this farce to continue."

Ronan could see that Brother Gilbert didn't have any ideas in reserve. A thought entered Ronan's mind, and before he could dismiss it, or even consider its merit, he stepped forward.

"Imagine how it would seem to Lady Sybilla," Ronan said thoughtfully, avoiding eye contact with his father. "The day she arrives, she hears the laird shouting most ungraciously at a fellow Englishwoman. Then she wakes the next morn to find that the young woman has been physically forced from Calder lands to journey alone for nearly a month."

"Certainly it would upset the lady, but I see not how that changes the matter for me," his father replied sharply.

"You would want my future wife to feel so uncomfortable, so unwelcome in her new home? And what would she think of her soon-to-be father and laird? Fear is all well and good, but we must ensure that our family feels safe," Ronan answered. He did not stop to consider the implications of his statement. He couldn't. If he had, he would have failed Adelina.

"Your future wife?" his father asked skeptically, "As I recall, Ronan Calder vowed very recently that he would never marry."

"Lady Sybilla would surely appreciate the company of a well-mannered fellow Englishwoman, noble or no," Ronan continued.

"You didn't answer me, lad," his father said. He looked for all the world like a cat who had cornered a mouse. "Do you intend to marry Lady Sybilla?"

"If you allow Adelina to stay, and to hold the position of scholar and all which that entails, then yes. I will marry Lady Sybilla before winter," Ronan conceded.

"Excellent!" Laird Calder rejoiced, his anger vanishing into thin air. A victory such as this was enough to banish any lingering malice. The laird retreated to his own private chambers deep within the keep, leaving Ronan alone with Brother Gilbert. Together, they slowly made their way down hallway and back into the great hall.

"Ronan," Brother Gilbert said in a tone filled with concern, "I hope you know what you're doing."

"He would've seen me married in the next year and you know it," Ronan replied defensively. "At least this way I am doing some good."

"It is only good if it is done for the right reasons," Brother Gilbert chided.

Ronan held up a hand. "I'm going to stop you there," he said sternly, "I've no need for a lecture on morals. I am simply trying to save the lass from a trying and unpleasant experience. You fought to keep her here, so you must believe she can do the job. I need no more reason than that to help her."

"You don't need any more reason, aye, but you have some. Be careful, Ronan. The lass may seem to be made of iron, but she can still be hurt," Brother Gilbert cautioned.

Ronan was tiring quickly of this conversation. "You waste your worries," he said, trying to end the discussion.

"I've simply had enough of young folk and broken hearts, 'tis all," Brother Gilbert said with a sigh.

"You sound like an old man," Ronan teased, changing the subject. What broken hearts had to do with anything was beyond his ken. He had no interest in marrying either of the women. His only problem now was figuring out how to get around that fact since he had just promised to propose.

Brother Gilbert smiled at him. "I am an old man, and I've earned the right to say as much. Which reminds me," he said, perking up, "Adelina will be taking over your Latin lessons beginning tomorrow."

Ronan stopped walking and grabbed Brother Gilbert's arm. "You can't be serious," he groaned, "she's but a young lass. I was a lad of six learning Latin before she knew her first words, by the look of it."

"Nevertheless," Brother Gilbert said with a chuckle, "she's far better at it than you. She'll be instructing you from now on."

"How can you possibly tell, in the short time she's been here, that she's qualified for such a task?" Ronan thought he made an excellent point. None of them knew her yet. She had only arrived that morn.

"She and I had a brief but lively discussion on the work of Dioscorides on our way to the keep," Brother Gilbert explained.

"Who?"

"Exactly," Brother Gilbert said with insulting finality. "Adelina will be an excellent tutor in the language. Arrive at the same time tomorrow, just after breaking your fast."

Brother Gilbert left without another word. Ronan stood, stunned, in the empty hall. What on earth had just happened? When he entered the building, he was a single man with a harmless attraction to a beautiful lass. Now he was betrothed, to a completely different lass mind you, with an attraction to Adelina that was becoming something of a problem. He had already broken an oath he made to himself nearly a decade ago for the lass. What was next if he couldn't get control of himself?

He had planned to avoid her and his troublesome attraction to her. Now that he was to be studying with her it looked like, for better or for worse, Ronan would be spending a good deal of time with Adelina Matheson.

Chapter Nine

October 18, 1136

Fury overtook Adelina as she sat down at the library's modest table the following morning. She balled up her fists to keep from screaming in frustration at the pigheaded laird. Oh, she had expected him to be insulted at her presence, angry even. What she had never once anticipated was the strength of her own reaction. Adelina thought it would be easy to smooth things over with the laird, convince him that she was up to the task, and have the whole problem sorted in one afternoon.

She flopped onto the table before her, feeling for all the world like a child throwing a tantrum. Why did men have to be such brutes? Why couldn't anyone just accept that she was an intelligent, capable woman?

She couldn't help but wonder just exactly what she was doing here. No one wanted her here. She had no friends, not even a distant acquaintance. Indeed, she was strongly disliked by everyone except Ronan and perhaps Brother Gilbert. She was English, living in Scotland, utterly alone. With alarming speed, Adelina dissolved from a fit of anger into tears of defeat.

The echo of the mid-morning bell reverberated from the nearby chapel. The bell tower, much smaller than the one at Oxford, sounded muffled and softer, as though it tiptoed through the hours. The gentle cling-clanging continued for a count of nine.

Nine! The sound brought Adelina back to the present. She straightened in her chair, wrenched from her self-pity. Ronan would be arriving any minute for his lessons. Suddenly flustered, she took a moment to clear her mind. Brother Gilbert had only informed her this morning that she would be instructing Ronan in Latin, beginning that very same day. Then he had promptly gone to say his prayers in the chapel, leaving Adelina to wonder exactly what was expected of her.

Several deep breaths later, Adelina had regained control of her emotions. She needed a plan. No matter what, she had to do a wondrous job this morning. More than anything, she had to prove to the laird that she was an asset to the clan. Helping Ronan with his Latin was her first chance, and she couldn't botch it. Word would certainly make its way from son to father that bringing her here was a terrible mistake.

The door opened just as Adelina decided on a way to begin her first trial as scholar. Ronan walked in, frowning. He looked ready to do battle, his muscles tensed across his shoulders.

"Good morning," Adelina said cheerily, hoping she had misjudged his mood.

He said nothing, but sat down in the chair opposite her with a grunt of acknowledgement.

"I wanted to thank you for being so kind to me yesterday," Adelina tried, "It meant a lot to have someone supporting me after such thorough humiliation."

"Don't mention it," he said sadly.

Mayhap he had a rough morning. Adelina decided to pay no mind to his poor mood, focusing instead on the task at hand.

"Of course," she replied. "What was the last thing you were reading?"

"I don't remember," he answered, refusing to look at her.

Adelina felt her temper picking up. To her it seemed much less that he couldn't remember and much more that he didn't care to tell her for some reason. She wasn't certain how much more she could take of his being difficult. Didn't he realize how important it was for her to do well today?

"Maybe I should just leave," he suggested, rising from his chair not two minutes after he'd first sat down.

Fire rose up from the pit of her stomach, refusing to be contained any longer. Adelina shot up from her own chair, placing her hands on the table and leaning toward Ronan, eyes narrowed.

"Now you listen here," she threatened, her voice low, "I can appreciate that mayhap you've had a bad morning. Mayhap you've even had a bad night. But you are not going anywhere. It is my job to teach you Latin this morn, and so we are going to get to work whether you like it or not."

Ronan sat back down in his chair, arms crossed, considering her for a moment. The corner of his mouth cracked into a reluctant grin. "Yes, ma'am," he replied.

Adelina was still worked up, and she wasn't buying it. "Are you making fun of me?"

Ronan leaned forward across the table to match her, so close that she could feel his breath across her face with each word.

"I never make fun of a lass who stands her ground," he assured her, his voice smooth and low.

Adelina's anger vanished. His intimate tone gave her shivers, and she had to pull back from him. She cleared her throat, then slowly walked toward the bookshelves, regaining her calm with each step.

"Now, let's try this again. What was the last thing you were reading?" she asked, running her hand absently along the spine of a particularly nice volume.

"Cicero's *In Catalinam*," he answered without hesitation, reclining in his chair once more.

Adelina burst into laughter. The irony was far too much for her after everything she had gone through over the last few days. She had traveled hundreds of miles only to arrive right back at Cicero. That man just couldn't leave her alone.

"What's so funny about Cicero?" Ronan asked, clearly confused.

"I –," she tried to explain, but a sputter of giggles choked out the few words she attempted.

Ronan waited, eyebrow raised.

"It's just – my brother," she managed, pulling Cicero's oration from the shelf and returning to the table. "He was reading through the same thing just before I left to come here."

Ronan looked at her with surprise. "You have a brother?" he asked.

"Of course I have a brother," she said matter-of-factly. "Doesn't everyone?"

"I don't." He folded his arms again.

Adelina sobered. "Oh, well you must have a sister, then," she suggested, trying to smooth things over.

"Can we just study Latin, please?" His tone suggested she drop the subject of siblings with all haste.

She sat down, opening the book. As she leafed through it, Adelina realized she hadn't seen or heard talk of any other family members since she'd arrived. His sensitivity to the matter made her wonder exactly why he had no siblings. Had something awful happened? He seemed grumpy today, so mayhap he was just generally belligerent.

"Where did you leave off with Brother Gilbert?" she asked, hoping he would lighten up again. She was absolutely determined to get through a lesson today. If she couldn't, how could she convince anyone of her worth as a scholar?

"Let me ask you something," Ronan said, completely ignoring her question.

Adelina huffed, crossing her arms. It seemed he insisted on being difficult today. Very well, she'd indulge him. But he wasn't leaving this room until he learned something of Cicero from her.

"Do you think Cicero really hated Catiline?" he asked. His eyes burned with intensity, and it was the most focused and interested he had been since he walked through the door. "Obviously he was furious with him for trying to overthrow the Roman Republic, but do you think on a personal level he truly hated him?"

Shock warred with amusement as Adelina considered his query. Realizing that the answer was more important to him than a history lesson, Adelina gave it quite a bit of thought before she replied.

"I think that Cicero *believed* he hated Catiline," she answered carefully, "But we are not always aware of our true thoughts and feelings. Maybe it was the same for him."

Ronan nodded his head, his hand on his chin, his eyes deep in his own thoughts. "Maybe Cicero really admired Catiline," he mused aloud.

"If he admired him, but claimed to hate him, mayhap he was jealous," Adelina offered.

Ronan immediately shook his head. "Nay, 'twas not jealousy. Catiline wasn't a good person."

Adelina considered his reaction. She didn't know him well enough to know exactly what he was talking about, and she dared not ask. He might stop talking altogether, and she could tell from his mood that he was sorting out something important. Taking a shot in the dark, Adelina guessed that mayhap he was at odds with his temperamental father.

"We don't know a whit about what type of a person Catiline was," Adelina argued, "He was a complicated man involved in complicated politics. When you're in a position of power like that, sometimes you're faced with difficult decisions. I am convinced that Catiline always did what he thought best in any given situation, even if it seems odd to us."

Ronan looked up at her, his hazel eyes filled with some unidentifiable emotion. He ran his hand through his hair, his gaze softening.

"Adelina," he began quietly. The creak of the old wooden door opening interrupted him.

A wave of disappointment rushed through her. Adelina turned to look at the door, wondering what he had been about to say to her so intimately.

A stunning young woman entered, looking around the room. She had hair so fair it looked as though she wore the sun itself, streaming in golden curls over her shoulders. Her almond-shaped eyes searched the room. She jumped a bit in surprise when she noticed Adelina and Ronan sitting before her. Somehow she had overlooked them.

"Oh, I do apologize," she said sweetly.

Ronan turned to look at the lady, his mood changing instantly.

Adelina had a sinking feeling in the pit of her stomach. She wiggled uncomfortably in her chair, afraid to ask what the woman was doing here. Why did she feel so anxious?

"'Tis no trouble at all, Lady Sybilla," Ronan answered her. "This is Adelina Matheson, our new scholar."

"Pleased to meet you, Adelina," Lady Sybilla greeted her. "I'm terribly happy to find another Englishwoman about."

"As am I," Adelina lied. She was anything but happy, though she couldn't for the life of her divine the reason. Normally she loved meeting new people.

"It is so progressive of you to offer such a position to a woman," Lady Sybilla complimented Ronan with a smile. "I wouldn't have expected such opportunity here."

Ronan opted not to respond to her comment, instead asking, "Is there anything I can help you with?"

"I was just having a look about the grounds," Lady Sybilla explained. "But I wouldn't turn down a guided tour, if you have the time."

"Of course," Ronan acquiesced, entirely too quickly for Adelina's liking. "I'm afraid we'll have to end our lesson here for the day," he said to her.

Sadness welled up in her chest, and Adelina simply nodded. What more was there to say? He was so taken with Lady Sybilla that he nearly ran out the door to be rid of Adelina. Had it been that awful? She had only been trying to do her job.

Would Laird Calder hear about how useless she was teaching Latin? She hadn't uttered a single word of it before her ill-tempered student had fled in haste. Damn it all, Adelina thought bitterly, wiping a single tear that had escaped down her cheek. Why had Ronan been so eager to get away from her? And why did she care?

As she watched them walk out into the midday sunshine, Lady Sybilla turned and took a long look at Adelina.

"I'll be back for you later, dear," she promised, her tone dripping like honey. Adelina thought that such an occasion would be anything but sweet.

Chapter Ten

"What affliction is going around today?" Brother Gilbert lamented the moment he returned to the library and caught sight of Adelina.

Startled, Adelina looked up from her musings. "I beg your pardon?" she asked.

"Oh, don't you start with me," he said tartly. "First Ronan barrels past me this morning looking like he's out for blood. Then I get back here and you're staring at my table like you want to fall into it. Is no one capable of moderation today?"

"Brother Gilbert," Adelina said, mustering her resolve, "I assure you I am perfectly fine." She couldn't repress a sniffle following her statement, which unfortunately lessened her credibility.

Brother Gilbert lifted an eyebrow questioningly, but thankfully withheld his comments. Instead he walked over to the window behind her and opened it, breathing deeply as the fresh air rushed into the stuffy room. It was a chilly day, the air crisp and clean with the promise of winter, a few short weeks away.

"When were you last out of this room?" he asked her as he gazed out toward the chapel.

Adelina shifted uncomfortably. "I don't see how that matters," she replied, skirting his question. She couldn't possibly tell him she hadn't left the library yet today. She had skipped breaking her fast, not feeling quite up to a meal with the grumpy old laird first thing in the morning.

"Sunshine is a gift," Brother Gilbert chided her, "God gave it to us for days such as this."

She bristled at his suggestion that something was wrong about her day. It didn't matter whether or not it were true. She shouldn't be allowing herself to be so transparent. "What do you mean, a day such as this?" she asked defensively.

"A day when we are filled with clouds of our own making," he answered, grabbing her hand and pulling her out of the chair. "Come, let me show you the keep's garden."

As they stepped outside, Adelina took a deep breath, letting the chilly breeze fill her lungs. She pulled her cloak tighter, taking a quick look around to see if Ronan or Lady Sybilla were in sight.

"This way," Brother Gilbert said, already ten steps ahead of her.

Adelina hurried to catch up to him. "Who tends the garden?" she asked, trying to take her mind off of the laird, his son, and Lady Sybilla. She still couldn't help but look around anxiously.

"You're going to trip over your own two feet if you don't pay attention," Brother Gilbert scolded her.

Her face reddened, yet still her mind wandered. "I simply wish to avoid any more problems today," she offered as explanation.

"Hmph," was all Brother Gilbert had to offer on the matter. They cut across a small alley behind the stables, past the blacksmith, and just out of sight of the keep's courtyard. The small holding was a bustle of activity, errand boys, horses, warriors, and women all going about their business. They rounded a corner behind the keep itself and Brother Gilbert opened an iron gate that led into a walled garden.

Adelina was greeted not by a verdant array of flowering plants, as one might expect in the fall, but rather a sad-looking display of withering chaos. The herbs and vegetables were tended well enough, but it was clearly not a well-loved space. Comfrey, calendula, feverfew, and tansy had perhaps thrived near midsummer, but their dried out forms were too far gone to be useful any longer. A lone red rosebush was making a heroic effort at a fall flush of blooms.

"I can see by your expression that it's not quite as you expected," Brother Gilbert observed lightly.

She searched several long moments for a gentle answer, but none came. Ultimately, she decided that brutal honesty was all she had. "It's dreadful," she stated flatly. Adelina ambled up and down the unkempt beds, hoping something promising might jump at her. Reaching the opposite end of the garden, she realized that perhaps she ought to begin her work here instead of in the library.

"I will admit," Brother Gilbert acquiesced, "the library has been my priority during my tenure here. I put all of my efforts into building Clan Calder up as a foundation of knowledge and history - a place where other scholars might venture to research and learn."

"So no one is tending the garden," Adelina murmured, answering her own question from earlier.

Brother Gilbert rolled his eyes. "I think you and I ought to have another chat," he said brusquely.

Adelina felt a flush rise to her cheeks, and she looked down at her feet. She had spoken too critically of his work while she wallowed in her own injured feelings.

"I do apologize, Brother Gilbert," she offered remorsefully, "You have created a wonderful wealth of knowledge in the library here. I wouldn't rightly expect you could also tend a thriving garden. I did wonder, though, why one of the servants, cooks, or ladies of the house hasn't been more attentive to this sad plot."

Brother Gilbert put his hand on her shoulder kindly. "Mistress Adelina, there is no lady of the house. 'Tis why Laird Calder pushes Ronan into marriage before he wills it."

Adelina's heart skipped a beat. The color drained from her face, and she once more had the same sinking feeling in the pit of her stomach as she had this morn. "So Ronan is to marry Lady Sybilla." It wasn't a question, but rather an assessment.

"Ronan is doing his clan a great service by marrying an English noble," Brother Gilbert explained, "I myself advised in favor of it."

Adelina felt tears threatening, and she turned away. What on earth was coming over her? She'd met Ronan only yesterday. She'd had, what, two conversations with him? And she was ready to fall over in a pile of sorrow because he was engaged to another woman. A beautiful, cheery woman, Adelina thought bitterly.

She couldn't explain it, not rationally. When she saw him her stomach fluttered with excitement, and she could hardly catch her breath. During the little time she had spent around him, she found herself wishing he were just a bit closer to her, admiring his muscular build and beautiful hazel eyes.

"I know 'tis not fair, lass," Brother Gilbert continued. "But 'tis the way of the world. Women such as Lady Sybilla were born to wed the sons of lairds. You and I, we have a different place in the world. Not better or worse, just different."

"Brother Gilbert, I wonder if I might have a moment alone in the garden?" Adelina asked politely.

"That does sound lovely," Lady Sybilla interjected, appearing in the garden with her maid before Brother Gilbert could answer. "Unfortunately, I'm here to collect you, as promised." She smiled broadly, offering her arm to Adelina as though Lady Sybilla were acting the suitor.

Dread piled from the pit of her stomach to the top of her chest as Adelina watched Brother Gilbert's black robes disappear through the gate and beyond the garden wall. She was alone with the other Englishwoman. A noblewoman, no less.

Chapter Eleven

"Oh, don't look so miserable Adelina," Lady Sybilla chided. "I only wish to spend time with my new friend. We Englishwomen must band together, you know."

Adelina was at a loss for words. An unusual occurrence, to be sure. Though Lady Sybilla played the part of a friend, Adelina had met enough nobles to know they could seldom be trusted. A friendly face and kind words often hid nefarious motives. What she could possibly be up to, Adelina couldn't fathom. Hopefully by the end of this miserable afternoon she would be better informed.

When it was clear that Adelina wasn't going to say anything, Lady Sybilla continued with introductions. "This is my lady's maid, Lucy," she said, gesturing to the woman beside her.

Lucy was of a middling height with her hair once more in a tight bun. She had a fair face and a pleasant smile, but she was clearly not of noble stock herself. Her skin was far too sun-darkened. Her linen dress was mostly hidden by a heavy woolen cloak. Adelina noticed a small embroidered emblem just inside the hood, a beautiful Scottish thistle flower and a little dagger. The work was skillfully done. Lucy curtsied politely when introduced to Adelina.

Adelina did the same, trying not to judge the maid as critically as she had the mistress. "'Tis a pleasure to meet you, Lucy," Adelina managed. "Your cloak is beautifully decorated," she said, indicating the emblem on the hood.

Lucy blushed, pushing it further from her neck. "Oh, thank you, Mistress Adelina. 'Tis so kind of you to say so," she replied. Adelina noticed the brogue in her voice for the first time. She was Scottish.

"Please," she said quickly, "call me Adelina. None of this 'mistress' nonsense."

Lady Sybilla grinned, clapping her hands together gleefully. "Oh, yes," she added, "I'm so glad you mentioned that. You must call me Sybilla as well, if we're to be true friends."

"Of course," Adelina agreed. Of everything Lady Sybilla had tried so far, dropping the honorific in her name was the best possibility of gaining some of Adelina's goodwill. "So what exactly is it you wish us to do?"

Lady Sybilla clung to Adelina's arm like a sleeve, pulling her from the garden and out into the village. "I just finished a wonderful tour of this charming little village with my Ronan, and I thought you might want the same, since you'll be living here as well."

Her Ronan. The words turned Adelina's stomach, but 'twas naught she could do about it. Lady Sybilla wasn't wrong. Adelina forced a smile that she knew didn't reach her eyes. "That sounds lovely," she ground out.

They strolled in blessed silence for several minutes, and then Lady Sybilla did, actually, give her a tour of the village. She pointed out the blacksmith, the tailor, the bowyer, the weaver, the brewer, the miller, the baker, and the butcher. Adelina grudgingly admired that Lady Sybilla introduced each craftsman or woman by name. She had to have met them only an hour or two ago with Ronan, and yet she remembered each one. Lucy bought a loaf of bread from the baker, and the ladies wandered to a stand of oak trees on the edge of the village, overlooking the Highlands beyond.

"Tell me, Adelina," Lady Sybilla ventured, "how is it that you came to be the scholar of Calder Keep? You'll forgive me, I'm certain, for being so forward, but it is quite unusual to have a woman advising a lord, even in Scotland."

Adelina bristled at the question, but didn't shy away from an answer. "The masters at Oxford asked me to come here in response to Laird Murdoch's request," she explained. "They knew 'twould be a challenge to get any of their students to come during so much political turmoil, so they offered me the position."

"But 'tis so dangerous to be here all alone during wartime," Lady Sybilla pressed, "Surely they must have offered you something in exchange for your services."

"As a matter of fact," Adelina replied, not caring one bit for Lady Sybilla's nosy assumption, "they offered to let me take courses at the university."

Lady Sybilla let out a low whistle. "My you must be quite something then," she commented, narrowing her eyes.

"What made you agree to a visit?" Adelina asked in kind. "Why would an English noble house ever entertain thoughts of marriage to a Scottish laird's son? I should think it difficult to gain King Stephen's approval of the match."

"Oh, the king owes my father more than one favor," Lady Sybilla said dismissively. "Besides, 'tis in his best interest to make a fast peace with the Highland clans."

Last December, King Henry I of England had died suddenly, leaving his throne contested. He had named his daughter Matilda heir, but she was in Normandy leading a revolt against him when he passed. 'Twasn't what you would call a strong claim, what with the revolt over lordship of Normandy.

The king's nephew Stephen, a popular English noble and close friend of Henry's, stepped in to claim the throne in place of Matilda. Twenty-one days after Henry died, Stephen was crowned King of England. One week later, King David of Scotland had marched on northern England. Though the Highland clans had mostly kept to themselves, the Lowlanders and the Welsh among others took advantage of the new king's weakness. Rebellions began popping up along all borders, and currently Stephen's military was stretched a bit thin.

Lady Sybilla was likely correct that he desired at least a temporary peace with Scotland, if only to deal with his other problems first. That being said, Adelina thought the Blakewell family had sworn an oath of fealty to Matilda, as ordered by Henry while he yet lived. Supporting Stephen would make her a traitor, or at least an oath-breaker. She considered saying as much, if only to make Lady Sybilla uncomfortable, but Lucy spoke up first.

"And what about you, Adelina?" Lucy asked pointedly. "Which king do you support?"

"Wouldn't it be a king or a queen?" Adelina asked, thinking she meant Stephen or Matilda.

Lucy shook her head. "Nay, not in England. No offense, my lady," she added, looking toward Lady Sybilla. "I mean in Scotland."

"King David put down the rebellion last year," Adelina replied, not certain why her English opinion on Scotland's king mattered to Lucy. "As he was appointed by our King Henry, and his only opposition is locked away somewhere, I'd say I support King David."

Lucy balled up her fists, but her voice remained calm. "Just because he was the victor doesn't make him the king."

Adelina chuckled, attempting to bring levity to the heavy talk of politics. "I'd say that's exactly what makes him king."

Lucy opened her mouth to argue, but Lady Sybilla held her hands up. "Enough of this talk," she declared, standing and smoothing out her billowing golden skirts, "I'm certain Adelina has more than enough of politics while she advises the laird. Now tell me, Adelina, what do you make of that atrocious little garden they have?"

They continued walking together back to the courtyard. Lady Sybilla filled the time with as many insipid comments as she could devise. Adelina had to listen to her go on and on over clothing, decorating, embroidery, and the like until finally she was able to pull away in the direction of her cottage.

Walking back to her one-room cottage in peace, Adelina felt a sense of renewed purpose. Let Lady Sybilla stay and deal with the politics, the rivalries, the chaos. Adelina would be safely studying Latin in the calm lecture halls of Oxford, unless something went horribly wrong in the meantime.

She was going to be the best damned scholar Clan Calder had ever had. She was going to get into Oxford. And she was not, by any stretch of the imagination, going to get hung up on a man she could never have. She would teach Ronan his Latin, be kind and courteous, and when she got her letter of recommendation she would get out of the way as quickly as possible.

Chapter Twelve

October 19, 1136

"Tis simply a harmless attraction," Ronan assured himself aloud. Until two days ago, Ronan had led a life of masculine simplicity. When it came to his relationships with women, Ronan relied upon St. Jerome's sage words: avoid it like the plague. Instead, he focused his efforts on improving Clan Calder's defenses and raiding their neighbors when necessary. He trained, he fought, he made plans with his father and other elders, hunted game, and very occasionally he sent gifts and letters to his niece, Beatrix.

Since the arrival of Adelina, he had been beleaguered by troubles with women. His father pushed him toward marriage. Nothing new, he thought bitterly, but it was far more burdensome this time around.

He paced the small solar. Once, years ago, he had spent hours in this room with his sister. The morning before she birthed his niece, she had sat in the corner chair. The sun had streamed in just the same as it was this day. He continued his walk across the room. Back and forth, over and over, as though he could walk his troubles right out.

His lesson with Adelina yesterday morning had been trying at best. His plan to be as uninterested as possible dissolved far too quickly in her presence. Indeed, in a matter of minutes she had him so deep in conversation that he had nearly told her about his mother, his sister, his niece. He had come so close to confiding his deepest fears in her that it terrified him. He had only met the woman two days ago!

Blessedly, Lady Sybilla had given him an easy escape before he could do something he might regret. Ronan knew he wouldn't always be so lucky. He needed a plan. Could he somehow manage to avoid her?

As though reading his thoughts, the door to the solar flew open and the object of his deliberations strode in. Her fiery hair fell in a long braid down to her hips. Her face was the picture of shock, staring straight at Ronan in adorable surprise.

Fighting his urge to walk over to her, Ronan broke the awkward silence first. "Can I help you?" he asked, folding his arms across his chest in an attempt to look intimidating. Mayhap he could make her uncomfortable enough to leave and spare him any temptation.

She worked her lips, searching for words. Ronan couldn't take his eyes off them. Soft and inviting, he was certain they would be delicious on his own. He shook the thought from his head and began walking in the hopes of taking his mind off such nonsense.

"This isn't the kitchen," she said finally, stating the obvious.

A smile tugged at the corner of Ronan's mouth. He looked at her, seeing the sincerity of her statement. The lass was terribly confused.

"Nay, 'tis not," he agreed. "'Tis the solar."

A blush, as pink as the apples ripening in the orchard, flooded her cheeks. She took a quick step backward toward the door.

"I'm terribly sorry to intrude," she apologized. The solar was reserved for the use of the family. Only invited guests were typically allowed entry. Her blunder was clearly making her uncomfortable.

Ronan approached her, noticing for the first time that she carried a small ceramic jar. Adelina saw him inspecting it, and quickly offered an explanation.

"'Tis a salve," she said, herself looking at the jar, "for Eby."

"The cook?" he clarified.

"Of course," she replied, recovering all at once from her shock. "What other Eby is there? 'Tis not that common of a name."

"The blacksmith's daughter is named Eby also," Ronan countered. "As is one of the stable kittens born this past spring."

"And you thought I was searching the keep for a stable kitten in need of a burn salve?" she questioned him, eyebrows raised.

This woman's spirit was as fiery as her beautiful locks. She took exception to his words at every opportunity, and he had to admit, he rather looked forward to it. Aye, mayhap he needed to prick her temper a bit more before aiding her. He took a step closer to her.

"It would make more sense for the blacksmith's daughter to have a burn, would it not?" he retorted.

Adelina rolled her eyes heavenward. "And why would I be looking for the blacksmith's daughter in the keep?" She, too, stepped closer.

"You tell me," he said, closing the last few steps between them. "And why would you be looking for the cook in the solar?"

That last statement did it. She thrust her jaw out defiantly, jabbing his chest with her finger to punctuate her reply. "Did it ever occur to you that my stumbling in here was pure accident? I'm not just wandering the castle grounds looking for ways to annoy you. Did you not consider that I simply happened into the wrong room?"

Her words struck Ronan unexpectedly. He pulled her into his arms, grabbing her finger off his chest and enclosing her hand in his. Her bluster cooled instantly, leaving her lips parted mid-speech.

"You are many things, lass," he whispered gruffly, "but annoying isn't one of them." Ronan's hand reached up to caress the delicate line of her jaw, his thumb outlining its edges until he reached her full, parted lips. They looked to be waiting just for him. "Enticing, bewitching, tempting, alluring. Take your pick," he breathed as he brought his lips to hers.

She tasted just as sweet as she looked. Desire welled up from deep inside, where he had long kept it buried to protect his heart. At first he brushed his lips over hers. He had every intention of giving her a tender kiss, a simple kiss. Mayhap even a good-bye kiss. That was until she started kissing him back.

Her breath caught in her throat. He thought for a moment that she might pull away, retreat from his unexpected expression of desire. But true to her nature, she dove right into the fire.

She pressed herself so tightly against him that he could feel every curve of her, awakening a need he had long sought to avoid. He teased her lips apart with his tongue, greedily tasting her until she let out a sultry sigh. Ronan pushed the kiss deeper and deeper until it threatened to rob him of all sense.

Reluctantly, he finally pulled away, her fingers still laced in the hair at the nape of his neck. Those lips of hers were bright pink now, swollen and full after such a thorough kissing. He couldn't fathom what he ought to say next, nor could he afford to contemplate what such a moment might mean over the coming days.

Her bright blue eyes, clouded with a desire to match his own, searched his face. She looked far too sad for a lass who was in the arms of a man.

"What of Lady Sybilla?" she asked, her voice shaking with emotion.

God, she was right. What was he doing? It was shameful enough that he had no intention of sharing a bed with his future wife. The least he could do was keep his hands off Adelina. Aye, for Adelina's own sake he should leave her alone. The last thing he wanted was to become too involved with a woman he cared for. And whatever his intentions were, it was painfully obvious that he did care for her.

"I'm not marrying for love," he replied, realizing it still didn't explain a thing to her.

"But you are marrying," she said sadly.

"Aye. I must," Ronan answered, his resolve growing. He had been weak, but he would not make the same mistake again. "The kitchen is across the great hall, through the other door."

Adelina said nothing, fleeing the room in search of Eby as quickly as she could without running. Ronan watched her go, unable to ignore the enticing sway of her hips and the shimmer of that red braid as she walked.

Ronan's thoughts grew grim once more as Adelina moved out of sight into the hall. Even if he could somehow convince his father to allow him to marry a common-born Englishwoman, which itself would be a feat worthy of legend, Ronan could never allow himself to marry for love. He would only be setting himself up for heartache when the lass died birthing a babe, just like every other woman in his life had before her. He wouldn't put her life at risk.

The greatest irony of all was that the only thing keeping Adelina at Calder Keep was his timely engagement to Lady Sybilla. If he broke the engagement, his father would surely have Adelina thrown to the wolves at the earliest opportunity, forcing her to make her way back to England alone through the wilderness.

Each thought drew him toward the same conclusion. Aye, he wanted Adelina Matheson. She was charming, beautiful, intelligent, and he looked forward to her company with sinful excitement. She had a way of talking that drew him into a conversation whether he willed it or no. But 'twas not a harmless attraction. Nay, the strength of his feelings for Adelina had the potential to cause a good deal of harm if he couldn't keep them in check. Ronan resolved to stay as far from her as possible, to save them both.

Five days passed painfully by, and Ronan managed to make good on his promise to himself to stay away from Adelina and the temptation she brought. Aye, she charmed him every morning at their lessons, but with a great effort of will he left every morning without touching her again. Everything was going smoothly until midnight on the fifth day. When the messenger arrived, change swiftly followed.

Chapter Thirteen

October 24, 1136

The clip-clop of hooves echoed hollowly across the cobblestone courtyard at midnight. The bell for matins, signaling the time for midnight prayers, had only just finished its eerie toll. Heavy fog was settling in just outside the window, covering all the keep and the surrounding lands in a blanket of thick gray mist.

Ronan's eyes shot open when the sound of an approaching rider rose up from the courtyard below. Standing slowly, that he might also listen to the activity unfolding outside, Ronan strode over to his window.

A heavy oaken door, presumably leading into the stables, creaked open, and Ronan heard the footfalls of the horse recede further into the night. No one had spoken a word, which meant one of two things. Either the guards were dead, which Ronan thought unlikely, or they knew the rider. Looking through his window, Ronan couldn't make out the man's identity.

He quickly threw on a linen shirt, wrapping his plaid over one shoulder and fastening it. There wasn't time to wrap it properly, so he also donned a pair of breeks. Ronan needed to get down to the hall with all haste, and he guessed he wouldn't be the only man in the room looking disheveled. Before he had finished lacing his boots, a loud knock sounded on his door.

"Laird Calder asks you to meet him in the great hall immediately," Gamlin, his father's manservant, fair shouted. Ronan would wager his birthright that his father hadn't "asked" for anything.

Gamlin knocked on the door again, impatiently.

"I'm on my way," Ronan shouted at him. Though he felt some measure of comfort knowing that the rider was someone familiar to the clan, trepidation coursed through him as he took the stairs two at a time down to the great hall. Messengers at midnight were rarely a good thing.

When Ronan arrived in the hall, John, the oldest of the clan elders, aside from his father, was already standing behind one of the chairs. Laird Calder paced before the dying embers of the night's fire, frustration knit into his brow. Moments later, Lowrance, another clan elder, arrived. John, Lowrance, and the laird looked just as thrown-together as Ronan, like men woken at midnight in a hurry.

"Where the bloody hell is he!" Laird Calder roared at no one in particular. Ronan could tell already this would be a meeting he'd not soon forget.

"He'll be here, laird," John soothed gruffly, "You know how he is."

Finally managing to pull his attention away from the grumpy old men in front of him, Ronan noticed another, younger man in the room as well. Leaning against a shadowed corner of the room, Ronan's cousin Colban Drummond waited. Colban lived several hours' ride to the north with his father's clan. When last Ronan had heard, the Drummonds and their brother clan, the MacMasters, were currently embroiled in a feud with both an English noble named de Beaumont and Clan MacCready. Surely only news of great import would lead Colban away from his clan in a time of need.

Dark circles under his eyes told Ronan that Colban had already had a long night. He hoped the lad had the stamina for the fearsome interrogation that was no doubt coming.

Some ten minutes later, Alan finally walked into the great hall, dressed in proper Highland attire. Clearly, he had not felt obligated to immediately attend to his laird's summons.

"God's bones, Alan, I said *immediately*!" Laird Calder shouted at the old man.

"One must look one's best, even at midnight," Alan replied calmly. 'Twas not the first time the laird had lost his temper with Alan.

Ronan waited calmly for the elders to finish having it out with his father. 'Twas something of a tradition, that they find good reason to argue, before finally addressing whatever business had drawn them together in the first place. If it went on too long Ronan would interfere, but 'twas almost never necessary.

"Colban, lad, get your arse out of that corner and tell us what happened," Laird Calder bellowed.

Colban, the poor lad, looked a bit in over his head. Ronan had never thought his youngest cousin had the temperament of a warrior. He was better suited to the priesthood, perhaps. He slowly made his way from his hiding spot into the center of the room, before the laird and the other elders. He cleared his throat and straightened his plaid, looking nervously at the men assembled before him.

"I was riding my route through the woods at the border, when I smelled death," Colban explained. "I followed the stench and discovered a newly-dead corpse not twenty paces off the road, hidden amongst the brush. 'Twas Ewan, one of our men. He left with my cousin Aidan MacMaster almost two years ago. Until I found his body, we hadn't heard from either one since. I also found this letter stitched into his plaid. 'Tis from Aidan, addressed to Laird Murdoch." Colban handed the sealed parchment to the laird while everyone processed his tale.

"What does the letter say?" John asked the laird.

Laird Calder broke the red wax seal, which had no imprint upon it, then swore roundly.

"What 'tis it?" Alan asked with a frown.

"'Tis in Latin," the laird replied, grimacing.

"Isn't Ronan studying the language?" Lowrance suggested, "Why not have him read it for us?"

"I can bloody well read Latin," the laird growled.

"Then what's the problem?" Lowrance asked.

"It refers to a traitor within the clan," the laird replied, "but I think there is more to it that I'm not understanding. The second half makes no sense."

Lowrance threw his hands in the air. "Then have your bloody son look at it. He's been studying with the priest, has he not?"

Ronan felt the weight of eyes upon him. Aye, he had studied the language, but 'twas trickier to solve than one of the riddles in tales of old. Each word could change the meaning of the whole. A letter of such import ought to be examined by an expert. He gave his father a sharp glance.

"I could have a look," Ronan offered, "but you know what I'm going to suggest."

"No," the laird said flatly, returning Ronan's glare, "Absolutely not."

"Will someone tell us what the hell is going on?" Lowrance, the most outspoken of the elders, cried.

"For something so important, where the wording of it is crucial to the message, we should bring in our scholar to review it," Ronan explained, never breaking his father's stony gaze.

"Fine," John agreed, "That's an excellent solution. Then we won't have any misunderstanding of it. Ronan, why don't you go fetch Brother Gilbert?"

A smirk slid across Ronan's face. He crossed his arms, leaning back against the wall. So his father hadn't consulted the elders when he replaced Brother Gilbert. Did they even know the old priest was leaving? In another situation, Ronan would have left his father to explain everything to the men. Given that it was well past midnight and word of a traitor to Clan Calder was in the air, he decided to sort it out quickly.

"First, Brother Gilbert was called away three days ago for a funeral, two baptisms, and a wedding in MacMaster lands. Second, Brother Gilbert has been recalled to his monastery and is no longer our clan advisor. Mistress Adelina Matheson is his newly-arrived replacement."

Everyone began speaking at once. Most in concern, some in protest, and Lowrance in outrage.

"That's enough!" Laird Calder bellowed. "I like it even less than you, I assure you."

"Laird, this is too grave a matter to leave in the hands of a woman," Lowrance complained.

"When will Brother Gilbert return from the MacMaster holding?" John asked, ever the voice of reason.

"He'll be back just before Samhain, but will leave shortly thereafter. I imagine he'll be here a matter of days," Ronan surmised.

"We can't wait for him," the laird stated grudgingly, "By Samhain 'twill be too late."

"What do you mean?" Alan asked, leaning forward to grip the table.

"The letter says the traitor plans to act at Samhain," Laird Calder explained. "If we are to believe anything about this, we have only a week to act."

The hall filled with weighted silence as the men considered the best course of action. Ronan dared not comment, lest he push his father to make a poor decision out of stubbornness and pride. Laird Calder had the best interests of his clan at heart, aye, but his pride would be his downfall.

"Hugh! Bothan!" the laird shouted, calling the two warriors from their post at the door. They stood before him seconds after his summons, ready to do his bidding.

"Fetch Mistress Adelina," he ordered, "And don't let her waste any time on womanly concerns. Carry her from her bed if you must. I won't be left waiting for her to make herself ready. We are ready, and we are waiting. I want her here in five minutes. Tell her it is time she made herself useful."

Ronan's stomach lurched. Such actions, coupled with such words, would surely terrify the lass over her fate. "Father," Ronan began his objection. But the laird held up a hand to silence him. Before Ronan had a chance at being heard, the warriors had left to wake the lass.

Chapter Fourteen

A rough knock on the door sounded hollowly through the small cottage. Adelina rolled over in bed, pulling the covers tighter about her. Then the shouting began, and another knock sounded. Adelina shot up in bed, sleep lost and covers dropped.

"Open the door, lass!" a man shouted, banging on her door furiously. "The laird needs you straightaway!"

Though her instincts told her she ought not open the door in the middle of the night for strange men, particularly in her nightclothes, her sense of duty got the better of her. Turning the lock the threw the door open, glaring daggers at the two men before her.

"I demand an explanation," she seethed through clenched teeth. The wind whipped her hair and nightgown into an icy frenzy about her.

"Calm yourself, lass. We're in a hurry, 'tis all. We'll not hurt you," one of the men said.

"That is not an explanation," she argued, "and I'll not be going anywhere until I've had time to dress properly for such a meeting." She turned to close the door and find her overdress. She'd need to braid her hair as well. She'd left it down to dry after a late-evening bath.

"We haven't time for this. The laird will have our hides," the other man said. "Lass, I'm so sorry to have to do this, but you ken how the laird can be when he's riled."

Adelina started to argue, but the next thing she knew, she was bobbing over a man's shoulder, just as he might've carried a sack of barley. They were out her door, rushing through the foggy village. The night air was bitterly cold, holding all the chill of the coming winter.

Confusion now warred with fear, threatening to rob her of all sense. She pounded on the man's back, refusing to be treated so roughly.

"I'm so sorry, lass. I wish there were a better way," the man next to her whispered quickly.

"What is going on!" she shouted, not really expecting an answer.

"The laird has summoned you with all haste. You're needed at a meeting of the council," the same man explained. "He said to bring you straight from bed."

"Of course he did," Adelina said wryly. The laird was an absolute brute. She'd need to speak with him about proper treatment of one's advisor.

When they arrived at the keep some minutes later, the warrior at least had the courtesy to set her down so that she could enter the meeting on her own two feet. She was mortified to be seen in her nightclothes, hair undone, barely awake enough to hold a conversation. But she'd be damned if she let any of the men waiting for her in the great hall know that. Head held high, Adelina walked through the great oaken doors and stepped into the dimly lit hall.

Some old man whistled at her, and she didn't even deign to glance at him. She did, however, catch Ronan's eye as she made her way toward the smoldering embers of the fireplace. The color drained from his face as he watched her every step. He only took his eyes off her long enough to glare at the old bastard who had whistled at her yet again.

Adelina doubted very much that Laird Calder had ever treated Brother Gilbert in such a manner. But she was no fool, and she recognized his rudeness for what it was: a show of power. He didn't want her to think for one moment that she had any advantage on him. Though it made Adelina burn with anger and shame, as long as she got her letter into Oxford, she'd do what needed done.

She stood, hands folded politely in front of her, soaking in what little warmth the remnants of the fire offered. It would not do for her to be shivering on top of all the other indignities. Though she felt a rush of calm upon seeing Ronan, knowing nothing truly awful would happen to her, she still worried over what might cause the laird to summon her in the middle of the night.

"Read this," the laird commanded, shoving a letter into her hands. Adelina opened it carefully, reading the Latin message. Her command of the language was nearly flawless, but she had some difficulty concentrating.

"Laird, you've made a mistake using her as an advisor. She'd better serve you in bed," one of the old men said crudely.

"Aye," another agreed. "Look at that bosom!"

A blush of shame burned Adelina's cheeks. She knew it wasn't uncommon for low-born women to be treated so barbarically, but her father had such wealth that until this very moment she had never before been subjected to such behavior.

"That's enough!" Ronan roared. Silence returned to the hall. "Let the lass read."

Adelina couldn't bring herself to look at Ronan, grateful though she was that he'd put a stop to her embarrassment. Instead she concentrated on the letter.

"It says there is a traitor here who plans to sabotage the Samhain celebration," Adelina explained.

"Tell us something we don't know," Laird Calder grumbled.

"Lass," the third elder addressed her. He hadn't spoken since she entered, quietly observing from a chair near the head of the central table. "Does it say who? Is it a clansman? Are there any details which might help us identify this traitor?"

Adelina looked at the letter again, going over each word with a mind to his questions. Ultimately she shook her head.

"It's rather the opposite," she answered, looking him in the eyes to show she was not afraid to give her opinion. "It says many things, but 'tis all quite cryptic."

"How do you mean?" Ronan asked curiously. He stood straighter and took a step toward her.

"The first two sentences are from Cicero's speech against Catiline. In the context of the speech, he's referring to Catiline's realization of failure. When Catiline knows he will lose, he starts taking everyone else down with him. And 'tis one of two times the author mentions fire in the letter," she explained.

"The next part is quoted from *The Song of Roland*, about Charlemagne's wars. 'Tis a popular song in Normandy and the south of England," she continued. "It speaks of treacherous heathens coming together, and implies that Clan Calder will be open to whatever attack is planned. At the end he writes to 'Beware the fires of Samhain.' The last line is incomprehensible. It looks like Latin, but it isn't."

"How do you know that?" another elder asked, his tone accusatory.

Adelina bristled at his doubt of her skills, taking a deep breath before she answered. "Because I know Latin," she replied, "and it doesn't look like that."

"So the traitor is a foreigner?" the first elder asked, the only one who hadn't remarked at her near-nudity.

"Nay," Adelina answered him, "It's unclear. It could be anyone outside the clan, foreigner or Scot."

"So what, exactly, can you tell us for certain?" one of the rude men asked.

"There is a traitor on Calder lands who plans to make trouble with fire on Samhain," Adelina surmised. "To understand more of his references and to decipher the last line, I would need to spend more time with the letter."

"That sounds like the frailty of females to me," the man who had commented on her bosom said, "If Brother Gilbert were here, he'd have sorted this out by now."

"I assure you, it's not," she countered brusquely. "If you knew your Latin better, you'd know as much without my aid."

The man pushed a chair angrily out of his way, moving toward her. Ronan was between the two of them in moments.

Adelina felt rage rising, unbidden. "If I am of so little use to you, may I at least be permitted to return to my cottage?" she asked Laird Calder.

His cutting reply left no further questions. "If you have so little interest in being the scholar of this keep, you can return to your England."

As the rude old men continued to debate the identity of the traitor and how best to handle the threat to their clan, Adelina shuffled closer and closer to the fireplace. The embers that had greeted her when she arrived had burned down to little more than smoking ash. The chill of the night crept into the hall, and she had to pull her arms around herself to keep warm. She considered waking a servant to tend the fire, but decided she needed to stay and listen so that she could keep up with future conversations on the matter.

The debate went on incessantly, back and forth over the same minute details. Adelina was certain it would be dawn before they reached a decision. Just before they agreed to set watches round the clock within the village, Adelina lost the battle against the cold. The bitter autumn air finally left her shivering in her threadbare nightdress. She did her best to hide her condition from the men, who seemed little affected by the temperature of the room or lack of a fire. Only one of them noticed.

Ronan, backing away from the conversation, removed his plaid and walked over to her, accompanied by snide remarks from the two rude men. Laird Calder, she noted, said nothing. He watched, his eyes furious, as Ronan wrapped his own plaid over her shaking shoulders.

Lord, was it warm. The heavy woolen plaid instantly rid her of any chill, and blessedly covered her from the men's eyes. She wanted to thank him, but wouldn't risk getting him into even more trouble over it. Instead, she looked at him gratefully, pulling the plaid tighter about her.

"Get out," Laird Calder growled at her.

Adelina had had more than enough of this meeting. She turned and made for the exit without a word. Ronan followed on her heels.

"And what do you think you're doing, boy?" Laird Calder shouted at his son.

Adelina had observed that he only called Ronan "boy" when he was raving mad. It was the second time she'd heard him do so.

Ronan stopped, staring down his father. "There is a traitor in this village somewhere. I will not allow a young lass in her underclothes to walk about at the dark of the night without escort. 'Tis asking for mischief."

He didn't wait for the laird to respond. Instead, he put his hand on Adelina's back and guided her gently out the door into the cool autumn night, taking the letter with him. Adelina was surprised that the laird didn't shout about that, but he seemed to understand that there was nothing more they could do with it unless Adelina helped them.

Ronan led her quickly through the sleeping village. A dense fog had settled around the glen in the short time they'd been in the keep, and Adelina was all the more grateful that he was by her side. She wouldn't have felt safe without him after such a night.

"I'm sorry, lass," he whispered as they snuck into her cottage. "You shouldn't have been treated thus, Englishwoman or not."

"The apology is not yours to give," Adelina answered softly. She opened the door to her cottage and turned to face him.

Ronan lingered, as though deciding whether to speak or act before he took his leave. Was he going to kiss her again? Lord, she hoped so, though she was mortified to admit such a thing. Adelina realized then that she still had his plaid, and he was likely waiting for her to return it. She shrugged it off her shoulders, but his hand stopped her.

"Keep it, lass," he said, fingering the wool at the base of her neck. "It suits you." He moved his hand sideways, wrapping one of her tight red curls around his index finger. He looked wistfully at the strand, then cupped the curve of her face once more, just as he had in the solar several days earlier.

She hadn't seen him since then, except at their lessons, and had assumed he regretted the whole conversation. She hardly blamed him. Adelina knew there could never be anything real between them.

Ronan took a step away, walking off into the night without a word. He stopped before he was out of sight, and turned to her, as though he'd thought of something at last.

"Wear your hair down tomorrow," he commanded, the corners of his mouth lifting into a mischievous grin.

Adelina watched him walk into the mounting fog, only closing her door when he was out of sight. Before climbing into bed and under her beckoning covers, Adelina made sure to hide the letter securely in her cottage. She had discovered a crack in the clay daub behind her bed. 'Twas large enough to slip something into, but not easy to spot at a glance. To conceal the crack completely, she pushed the bed over even further and fell gratefully on top of it.

When Adelina closed her eyes, she saw Ronan, his hand gently grabbing a strand of her hair. If Ronan Calder asked it of her, she would wear her hair in curls for the rest of her days.

CHAPTER FIFTEEN

October 25, 1136

Ronan tugged gently on the straps of the saddle, checking that all three horses were ready to go. He couldn't get the image of Adelina from his mind. That red hair of hers, aye 'twas enough to tempt a man to sinful thoughts. Too sinful, he had determined.

He wasn't under any obligation to Lady Sybilla, particularly since they were not even technically engaged yet. He had promised his father, aye, but not a word had he spoken to the Englishwoman of it.

Nevertheless, he knew he would never be able to marry Adelina, so daydreaming about her fiery tresses spread across his bedcovers wasn't just pointless; it was dangerous.

And yet, he couldn't help but admire her. She was the smartest woman he'd ever met, and he'd wager she was smarter than most of the men he'd met as well. Of all her wonderful qualities, which he found himself contemplating more and more often these past few days, her fiery courage was what enthralled him. And mayhap the sway of her hips.

Before Ronan could finish his litany of praises, the stable doors opened and his riding partner for the afternoon walked in.

"I was so pleased to receive your invitation," Lady Sybilla said with a smile. "I was beginning to worry if I'd leave Calder lands without ever having spoken with you."

"I'm sorry it's taken me so long to invite you for a proper outing," Ronan said. He should feel sorry over it, he knew. But, Lord help him, he couldn't care less.

Lady Sybilla was finely dressed for her autumn ride through the countryside. Her sable cloak and heavy woolen dress would keep her warm in the face of the merciless winds that roved the Highlands this time of year. Unbidden, an image of Adelina in nothing but her nightgown came to mind. Just last night she had faced the same cold with barely a stitch of clothing. Had she slept in Ronan's plaid?

"My lord?" Lady Sybilla had walked over to one of the horses, ready to get going. Ronan hadn't even noticed that she'd moved.

"Won't your maid be coming as well?" Ronan asked. It wasn't proper for him to take a noble lady out without her chaperone.

"Oh," she replied, "I thought it might be more fun without her." Then she winked at him. She *winked* at him.

Lord, this ride was going be a trial of his patience, he could tell already.

They passed through the village just after midday. The mass of faces seemed like an endless blur of browns and pinks as Ronan desperately tried to find anyone with long, red hair. He remembered that he had asked Adelina to wear her hair down today. If she was out and about, he didn't want to miss it.

Lady Sybilla delicately cleared her throat next to him, demanding his attention. Ronan turned to her and smiled as best he could.

"She was called to one of the outer villages this morning," Lady Sybilla remarked helpfully. Guilt slammed him in the chest like a fist. She had known exactly who he was looking for.

"How do you know that?" Ronan knew he should be apologizing. He apparently had no restraint today.

She shrugged her shoulders, her furry mantle wiggling with the movement. "I pay attention," was all she offered as an explanation.

At a sudden loss for words, Ronan sped his horse up so they might get out into the hillside quicker. For a time, Lady Sybilla was content to ride in silence.

The bustle of the settlement faded into the distance as they crested the first true hill. In the Highlands, there were hills, and then there were *hills*, something not quite a mountain yet far too grand to be summarized by such a simple word. A group of men hauled long cabers up the steep slope, followed by women with bundles of sticks strapped to their backs.

"What are they doing?" Lady Sybilla asked, turning to get one more look at the group before her horse crested the hill.

"'Tis Samhain in a week, lady," Ronan replied.

Lady Sybilla widened her eyes meaningfully. She must not be familiar with the holiday.

"'Tis a festival for the harvest, the end of the season," he explained. "This week the last of the cattle will come down from the Highland pasture to winter near the settlements. Farmers harvest their oats, and drovers ready the cattle they mean to sell in the south for grain."

She nodded, carefully considering his words. "Then what's the lumber for?" she asked.

"On Samhain eve, great pyres are lit on the hillsides. 'Tis an ancient tradition to ward off ill spirits and purify the cattle," Ronan said.

"Purify?" Lady Sybilla's tone of disbelief was not lost on Ronan.

He smiled. "More like a blessing," he added. "Mostly 'tis an excuse for whiskey and dancing."

"In that case, count me in," Lady Sybilla said sweetly.

They rode on, the green of the pine forest peeking just over the next ridge. Ronan could smell the trees before he could see them. Closing his eyes, he reveled in the feel of the breeze and the scent of autumn. If only Adelina were here with him. She would love such an outing. Though she'd like as not be trying to teach him Cicero the entire way.

"Does everyone join in the celebration?" Lady Sybilla's question interrupted his thoughts.

"How do you mean?" Ronan asked. Was she wondering about Brother Gilbert? Perhaps she thought them truly pagan. He should have explained it better.

"Wouldn't you still need to keep warriors posted at each settlement? They'd have to miss out on the fun," she observed keenly.

Ronan nodded, wondering at the strangeness of her question. "Aye, we'll have warriors on the watch with nary a drink nor lass," he agreed. "I wouldn't worry over them, lady. They know what is expected of them."

Lady Sybilla smiled. "Of course," she replied quickly.

Not many women would be thinking of the whereabouts of warriors on a night like Samhain. But then, Lady Sybilla had been raised to manage a household. Ronan supposed that meant knowing everyone's whereabouts, including the warriors. Still, he couldn't quite shake the strangeness of her question.

The letter's warning came to his mind at the mention of fire and Samhain, but he quickly disregarded such nonsense. A gently bred woman couldn't possibly be behind such nefariousness. "You've quite a lot of questions about fire and guards, my lady," Ronan said.

"Oh, 'tis just a girl's foolish fancy, I suppose" Lady Sybilla said with a grin, "And my maid has been no help at all. she's Scottish, you know, but she hasn't explained any of this to me yet. She said 'twould be better to ask you."

They reached the edge of the great pine forest that sat right in the middle of Calder lands. It gently sloped downhill until the trees gave way to a quiet loch. Ronan thought Lady Sybilla might enjoy the scenic ride, and turned down the path leading deeper into the trees.

"I'm surprised it isn't Mistress Adelina you're taking into the woods," Lady Sybilla observed rather suddenly.

Ronan was instantly uncomfortable. He shifted in his saddle, but it didn't help much. Apparently Lady Sybilla wasn't one for subtlety. Lord, what could he say to *that*?

For the moment, he was spared. Lady Sybilla smiled at him wryly, looking at him out of the corner of her eye. "No need to fret, Lord Calder," she soothed, "I intend no judgment. We are not yet betrothed, and I am well aware that you have little mind for marriage."

Ronan felt a warm flush in spite of the chill breeze winding through the towering pines. He ran his hand through his hair anxiously. "I'm sure I don't know what you mean," he replied.

"Word travels quickly," she explained. "If I've heard correctly, your father has brought at least three other women here to tempt you to marriage, and you've cast each one aside. I have also heard that you and your father have come to something of an arrangement with regard to our betrothal."

"Where are you getting your information?" Ronan demanded.

"Are you saying it's false?" she countered.

"Well, not exactly," Ronan began.

"I care not what happens between you and the little academic," she interrupted, unsympathetic to Ronan's clear discomfort, "I have never expected to be my husband's first conquest. But I'd like us to come to an understanding."

Good Lord, what could she possibly have in mind? Ronan managed to clear his throat, finally finding his voice. "What sort of understanding?" he asked with growing concern.

The shock of her frank speech was wearing off, though he still hadn't a clue what to make of it. What sort of a lady spoke of such things with a man who wasn't even her betrothed yet? For heaven's sake, he hadn't even spoken so openly to Adelina.

"I don't need to know anything about your premarital activities," Lady Sybilla answered without batting an eyelash, "but once we're wed, I want you all to myself. And often."

Ronan thought he might die of mortification. It was highly inappropriate to have this conversation at all, let alone with an unwed, un-chaperoned noble woman. By God, he had to end this quickly.

He opened his mouth, hoping to placate her for the time being, but was robbed of the opportunity. Her horse bolted, racing at a dangerous clip into the thickening trees.

Ronan's heels dug into Sólas' side, urging him into a gallop. Lady Sybilla's mount was a well-tempered mare, and shouldn't have run off. In the back of his mind, Ronan's thoughts raced. What had spooked the gentle beast? He hadn't seen a thing.

For a rather round mare, Lady Sybilla's horse was giving a fine chase. Sólas tore through the narrow trail, until he came to a fork.

Ronan had no clue which way her horse went, and couldn't determine which of the many hoof prints were hers. A shout sounded up the hill to his left. Sólas ran.

There was still no sign of Lady Sybilla or her horse. Ronan searched through the trees, trying to catch sight of the lower trail in case he had taken a wrong turn at the fork.

He felt something push hard against his chest, propelling him backward off his stallion. The last thing he saw was a blue-gray sky.

Then the world went dark.

Chapter Sixteen

The words made no sense. Adelina would wager that the longer she stared at them, the less progress she made on deciphering the final line of Aidan's mysterious letter. Her mind felt like mushed oats, spilling all over the place without any focus at all. 'Twas most unlike her to have difficulty with her studies.

She had the letter before her on the library's small trestle table. Next to it she had Cicero's speeches, and she had at least managed to locate the lines Aidan quoted in his letter. Which wasn't at all helpful, as it turned out. Cicero simply went on and on about Catiline being a traitor who would murder everyone and destroy Rome. Which was all well and good, but didn't give her any more context for figuring out how to stop their very own traitor.

Adelina knew with a certainty that the most important line was the one she could not read at all. The identity of the traitor, or some key to stopping the plot, must be there in some cipher she couldn't deconstruct. It didn't help, of course, that her thoughts constantly strayed to Ronan as she attempted to work.

Oh, Ronan. She sighed so heavily that dust floating in the sunlight before her swirled like a glittering wave. What was she going to do about him?

One minute he was ignoring her, and the next he was kissing her.

The sound of male voices crept inside her window, interrupting her peace and quiet.

Adelina tensed. Her ordeal last night had been one she would prefer to forget sooner rather than later. She had forced herself not to think on the rudeness of the laird and the elders of the clan so that she could squeeze some sleep into what had remained of her night. How dare they treat her like a common whore? 'Twas the laird's fault, not Adelina's, that she attended the meeting in her nightclothes.

Her cheeks flushed and Adelina could feel her pulse picking up. She took several deep breaths, inhaling the familiar scent of the manuscripts before her. It was a waste of valuable time to let their poor behavior ruin her afternoon. She had but days to give the laird the information he needed to protect the clan, and so far she was failing utterly at her task.

Picking up the letter once again, Adelina glared at the line in question, as if she could demand it to give up its secrets. Once again, no such luck.

As Adelina worked, her thoughts continued to lead her to Ronan. After last night, she found herself hoping he would come to call on her. Her hair had been down since she woke, as he requested. Though she'd gotten several sideways glances, none had been from the handsome warrior.

More than once, she'd imagined what it would be like to share more than a kiss with him. He was so kind to her, especially compared to everyone else aside from Brother Gilbert. And good Lord those muscles! She wagered 'twould take more than two of her hands to encircle his arms. Not that she'd ever find out.

For as much as he dallied with her, Adelina knew it could never be more than that. She was common born, and English on top of it. He was soon to be betrothed to the fair and delicate Lady Sybilla. How Adelina wished she could be so elegant.

She stared down at the letter but didn't register it. Her mind was too occupied by her personal turmoil, as much as she tried to ignore it. Should she put an end to it? Should she keep living in temptation, never knowing what to expect at their next meeting? Did she have any other options?

Deciding she needed a break, Adelina stood to look through the library once more for *The Song of Roland*. She knew it would be nothing short of a miracle for a copy to be so far north, but with the library's reputation, she held out a glimmer of hope. Not to mention Aidan knew it well enough to quote it, which meant he had read it somewhere. Why not here?

And then it struck her. The moment she stepped between the first set of shelves, it was as though she'd been hit by lightning. She knew exactly what to do about Ronan. What if she went along with the fantasy? What if she just let herself enjoy the next few months of her stay at Calder Keep? She could happily pretend that they were lovers about to be married, no matter how far it was from the truth.

She would indulge her feelings for him. And when the time came for him to marry Lady Sybilla, she would have her letter into Oxford and be gone. He didn't seem bothered by her common birth. Why should she be?

"Mistress Adelina?" A woman's voice called to her, pulling her attention swiftly from her own thoughts.

She was tall and slender, her dark hair pulled into a neat bun. Adelina recognized her as Lady Sybilla's maid, Lucy. Her face was flushed from exertion. She ran right over, grabbing Adelina's arm and pulling her toward the keep.

"What's the matter?" Adelina asked.

"The laird's son," Lucy said quickly, "he's hurt. Badly."

Adelina's stomach lurched. Ronan was hurt. And it was serious enough they sent a lady's maid running for help. Once her statement had sunk in, Adelina hurried to grab the letter before leaving.

"What's that?" Lucy asked. "Where are you going?"

Adelina had turned away from the keep, toward her own cottage. "'Tis nothing," she lied, not wanting to scare Lucy with the truth, "Just a letter I'm helping the laird with. But I need to see it safely back to my cottage before I can go anywhere else. He'd be furious if I lost it." That much was true, at least.

Several minutes later, Lucy waited outside her cottage while she safely stowed the letter, and together they rushed to the keep. Adelina knew she was the best healer that Calder had seen in a long while, but she was by no means well-trained yet. She only hoped that she knew enough to help him.

Ronan's room was absolute chaos. If Adelina hadn't been so concerned for his life, she'd have burst into laughter. Lady Sybilla, now joined by her maid, were positively fussing over Ronan, who was lying in bed looking exhausted. He wasn't too ill to be angry, though. His nostrils were flared and his jaw was tight. He was fuming mad. Two warriors, likely the men who had brought Ronan to his room, hung around trying to be useful and trying not to stare too long at the beautiful women fawning over their lord.

Adelina cleared her throat. Five pairs of eyes pinned her against a wall.

"Thank God," Lady Sybilla said, her voice filled with concern. "Mistress Adelina, they say you are a skilled healer. Please, please help Ronan. I don't know what to do."

"Thank you for your confidence, my lady," Adelina replied, trying to sound calmer than she felt. "First, I'll need to know exactly what happened. Who was with him when he was injured?"

"I was," Lady Sybilla replied. "We were riding in the woods outside the village. My horse started, and he chased after me, but somehow we were separated. I didn't see what happened to him exactly. Once I managed to calm the poor beast we wandered the trails until we found him. He was lying on the ground, his horse a good mile farther down the trail grazing. He'd been thrown and landed on a log, I think."

Jealousy raged through Adelina. Ronan had been on an outing with Lady Sybilla while she had been pining away for him. The irony of it stung, but she shouldn't have been surprised. After all, he was expected to spend time with the woman if they were to be betrothed. She knew he was only doing his duty, but it somehow didn't hurt any less. It took her a moment before she felt composed enough to respond.

"Thank you, Lady Sybilla, for your succinct retelling. Now, everyone needs to leave," Adelina ordered. Lady Sybilla hesitated. "I'm sorry, my lady," Adelina explained, "When there is a head injury, quiet is best. He needs to rest his mind."

Lady Sybilla bristled, but agreed. "Very well," she allowed, "but I wish to be updated on his progress as soon as possible."

"Of course," Adelina assured her. She quickly cleared everyone else from the room, sending Lucy to the library to retrieve the supplies she needed to care for him. When she returned, Adelina went about cleaning and inspecting the wound on his head.

"Ow!" Ronan shouted.

Adelina rolled her eyes. "You sound surprised that a gaping wound on your head hurts," she commented.

"Aren't you supposed to be kind and reassuring to your patients?" he asked, cringing as she cleaned the dirt from the gash on his scalp.

"It depends on the patient," she answered cooly, "When I expect trouble from them, I find a firm hand is best."

"You expect me to give you trouble?" Ronan teased.

"Always," she retorted. "What knocked you from your horse?"

Ronan hesitated. She thought perhaps he was embarrassed. An injury from riding wasn't as most dramatic as a battle wound, to be sure.

"I didn't see," he said at last. "I was searching the tree line in case I had missed her somewhere. I did feel something hit my chest, but I never saw a thing."

"What could hit your chest, hard enough to knock you from your horse, but not leave a mark?" Adelina asked. Satisfied with her inspection of his head wound, she moved around to have a good look at his chest. There was no damage to his clothing, but that didn't mean he was unscathed.

"A rope," he replied, pressing his lips into a line of frustration. "I was moving so fast, looking the other way. Even if I'd seen it I might not have been able to stop."

That sounded entirely plausible, but it was far more concerning than relieving. "Do you think the traitor is at work already?"

"Aye," Ronan replied, "I do now. And I'm more the fool for not being careful."

Adelina considered the day's events, wondering if perhaps they contained some clue of who might be the traitor. "Lady Sybilla was the only other person out riding with you, when you were thrown from your horse," Adelina pointed out.

Ronan nodded with a grimace. "'Tis true," he agreed grudgingly, "but I've no idea how she could have managed it. Come to think of it, she was saying a lot of odd things while we rode. Her horse started off out of nowhere as well."

"Perhaps we should mention that to your father," Adelina said.

"Nay," Ronan replied hesitantly, "I think we should look into it more ourselves first. 'Tis a bold accusation to bring forward on nothing but conjecture."

Adelina agreed, but she needed to get on with her examination. They could talk more of the traitor once she was certain Ronan would be alright. "I need you to take your shirt off," she said, changing the subject entirely.

Ronan grinned. "I thought you'd never ask."

Adelina's cheeks were suddenly hot. She hadn't even considered how that might sound. "Don't get too excited," she replied, "I have to give you an examination to be sure nothing else was injured in your fall."

Ronan's gaze went to her hair, falling in red spirals around her shoulders. Just as he'd asked.

"You wore your hair down," he commented, twisting one of her bright locks around his hand. Just as he had last night.

Lord he smelled good. Somehow sweet and masculine all at once. She could feel herself moving physically closer to him, drawn into his arms.

"Your shirt," she whispered. Tempting warrior or no, Adelina was determined to be certain he was healthy other than the wound on his head.

In one swift movement, he pulled his shirt over his head. Adelina's breath caught, and she knew she was staring. His chest, his stomach, all of him was solid muscle.

"'Tis how I feel when I see your hair, lass," he said, his voice low. "Or when your dress catches the curve of your hips when you walk away from me."

He kept one hand in her hair, caressing it as he moved to hold the nape of her neck. She ran her hands across his strong, broad chest, feeling the bands of muscle beneath his warm skin. His other hand grabbed her hip, squeezing pleasantly. Then he pulled her lips to his.

Adelina lost herself in his kiss. When he had stolen a kiss from her in the solar, it had been exciting. This was devouring. His mouth moved over hers with such passion she could hardly breathe. And yet, somehow, it wasn't enough.

She grabbed his shoulders, massaging them beneath her hands, grasping for something she couldn't name. He growled, wild with lust. His tongue danced across her own, inviting her, tempting her.

His hand moved up along the curve of her hip, up until his thumb was brushing the side of her breast. She moaned, and that was all the encouragement he needed. He cupped her, gently at first. When she arched into his hands, he started moving her dress aside.

Adelina pulled back from the searing kiss just for a moment, just to catch a breathe before plunging back in. At least, that was her intention, until she noticed his eyes. They were circles of solid black.

Her passion dissipated instantly, replaced with deep concern. He noticed.

"What's wrong?" he asked, his voice husky.

"Your eyes," Adelina answered. The injury to his head had done damage on the inside as well, just like Gemma told her about so many weeks ago. "You need blackberries."

CHAPTER SEVENTEEN

October 26, 1136

Adelina posted two warriors to look in on Ronan throughout the night, since she wasn't exactly welcome inside the keep,. She knew that during his first night with such an injury, he needed to be woken periodically. Gemma had said that for some reason, whenever the mind was shaken, the first night of recovery was the most critical. Since she could do nothing more than let him rest, she returned to her cottage for a fitful night of sleep.

The following morning, an icy breeze sent shivers into her bones. Adelina pulled Ronan's plaid tighter about her shoulders and rolled over in her bed. It smelled just like him. She inhaled deeply, sighing in her sleepy haze. Good Lord – Ronan!

Adelina shot from her bed like an arrow from a crossbow. She had to check in on Ronan, and she needed to get going. Her cottage was a good stretch of the legs through the settlement. She walked over to the little table she had been sitting at last night, going over the letter yet again. She'd tucked the letter away, but the other documents had been left out. The moment she looked at the tabletop, all thoughts of Ronan fled her mind.

Someone had been in here. *While she slept*. Everything had been tidy when she returned from tending Ronan last night. This morning, Cicero's orations were torn to pieces, scattering across the rush-covered floor with each step she took.

Another breeze sent a shock of cold into her cottage. Pages skittered. She felt utterly exposed. Someone had opened her windows and snuck inside. By some stroke of unimaginable fortune, they hadn't harmed her. Why would someone break in, destroy her books, and leave her untouched? It was the same thing she had wondered about Ronan's riding accident. Someone had knocked him from his horse, clearly trying to kill him. And yet, while he lay on the ground the person had taken down the rope and left. Why hadn't Ronan been killed after falling?

She hurried to put on her clothes and get as far away as she could from her cottage, her mind reeling. Adelina needed to get away. The thought of how close she had come to danger crept over her skin like a spider.

On her way out, she walked over to the windows to pull the shutters closed. As a matter of habit, Adelina peeked around the village just outside her cottage, and happened to see Lady Sybilla.

It was odd, her being out here so far from the keep where she was staying. Even stranger, though, was the fact that she was alone. Lucy was nowhere to be seen.

Quickly shuttering the windows, Adelina rushed out the door with her healer's satchel, Ronan's plaid wrapped about her like a shawl. Like a gigantic, warm shawl that smelled just like the handsome warrior. She inhaled again. He'd better be alright, or she'd have a few things to say to him. As it was she craved the comfort of his company. At least she would be safe while she was with him.

When she began her walk through the village up to the keep, Adelina had been hurrying to see Ronan as quickly as possible. After several minutes in the chill autumn air, Adelina was hurrying to get indoors as quickly as possible. The temperature had dropped considerably overnight, and she was in no great hurry to catch a chill. Hopefully it warmed again before Samhain.

The keep loomed before her as Adelina climbed the small hill leading up into the courtyard. Stark grey walls hovered above, as though they could intimidate her into turning away. She pulled the great oaken door to the great hall wide open. It took her eyes a moment to adjust to the darkness of the room, lit only by a roaring fire. Apparently she wasn't the only one who thought it was too cold to keep the windows open.

"What are you doing here?" a voice boomed.

Adelina jumped. She'd been in such a hurry that she hadn't realized anyone else was in the room. The laird's anger was unmistakable. Had she done something wrong?

"Good morning, laird," she greeted him, pretending like he hadn't just bellowed at her in anger for existing. She walked through the room, headed for the hallway leading into family's quarters.

Laird Calder took three giant steps from his position in the shadows next to the fire, situating himself between Adelina and the hallway.

"I asked you a question," he said, crossing his arms.

Frustration threatened to get the better of her, but Adelina made herself take a deep breath. 'Twas only a moment of her time, and then she could check on Ronan.

"I'm here to check on your son," she replied coolly, "He was injured badly yesterday, and I need to ensure he's recovering."

She took a step to the side, as though to walk around him. He matched her, remaining between her and the way to Ronan.

"You won't be going anywhere near my son," Laird Murdoch intoned, his voice dripping with venom.

Adelina filled instantly with anxiety. "Is he alright?" she asked hurriedly. "Did something happen overnight?" Perhaps Ronan had taken a turn for the worse, and Laird Calder was guarding him out of fear.

"Nay, lass. Ronan is fine. *You* are the problem." He took one slow step toward her.

Adelina backed up, so she wasn't too close to the grumpy laird. What was wrong with him?

"I don't know what game you're playing," he growled, continuing to force her retreat, "I have to wonder now if a clever lass from England was sent here to undermine me. I saw him give you his plaid. I saw the way he looked at you. You're working my own son over, turning him against his future wife. No one knows where you were when he was injured on his ride."

She nearly laughed at the ridiculousness of the situation. Did Laird Calder truly believe she had been behind the mishap? "Laird, I assure you," she began, but his roaring voice cut her off. He had forced her nearly out the door as he took step after step toward her.

"I won't hear any of it!" he shouted. "How do I know you yourself didn't plant the letter we received, telling of a traitor? Perhaps you believed it would make you appear more skillful than you are, that you could read it. Perhaps you are the traitor, and sent it to cast suspicion upon another."

Adelina was growing desperate. For the first time, in her history of poor interactions with the laird, she was nervous. If he truly believed her guilty of treachery, he could have her killed. And to make matters worse, the real traitor would still be at large and no longer under suspicion. Calder Keep would be ripe for the picking.

"Laird, please," Adelina pressed. She had to see Ronan. She had to convince Laird Calder of her innocence.

"Enough!" he screamed at her, taking one final step to see her back out the door. Several servants and villagers were pretending not to watch the scene unfold. Likely the entire settlement would soon hear the tale. "I don't know what game you're playing, but I do know that you won't be allowed anywhere near my keep. I don't want to see you in here again." With that, he pulled the door shut in her face.

Adelina jumped backward just in time to avoid a broken nose. How was she going to help Ronan now?

Chapter Eighteen

Deep breaths. She had to take deep breaths. The cold air felt like pinpricks in her chest, but she knew she needed to calm down. 'Twas a good thing Ronan had given her his plaid, else she'd have been shivering by now.

That monster of a laird was proving more and more difficult. Fat tears of hopelessness threatened to spill from her eyes. What if she couldn't convince the laird she was no traitor? What if she never got her letter to Oxford? What if she couldn't get inside the keep to see Ronan?

One warm tear slid traitorously down her cold cheek, and she swiped it with her sleeve before any of the onlookers noticed. She might be on the verge of breaking down, but damned if she let anyone else see that.

Using the plaid to shield her from prying eyes, Adelina hurried out of sight. Where could she go? She didn't want to stumble into the beastly laird again. She needed time to make a plan, and she needed to be alone. As though her feet did the thinking for her, she looked up and realized that she had walked straight to the garden gate.

Finally alone, Adelina collapsed against the wall inside the garden, surrounded by herbs and weeds. She could no longer keep her tears at bay. They fell, like so many drops of rain, down to her chin. She sniffled, wishing her father were here to offer his advice. He always gave her good advice. At this point, she'd even take Brother Gilbert's advice.

"What's the matter, lass?" Eby had stepped out from the kitchen to pick some fresh herbs. Concern was etched into her face as she walked over to where Adelina sat.

"How can I help you?" the cook asked sincerely. Her kindness was a warm breeze on this chilly morn.

"I'm afraid you can't help, Eby," she uttered sadly, "Though I do appreciate the offer."

Eby was undaunted. "Try me," she pressed. "You healed my hands. I can't tell you how badly they pained me until you brought that salve. Now let me return the favor."

A glimmer of hope lifted Adelina from despair. She looked up at Eby. "I have an idea," she said.

"I sure hope it involves me making a scene," Eby said cheerfully.

Violent screams erupted from the kitchen. Eby cried out like her life depended upon it. She wailed and hollered until the laird himself came in to see what all the raucous was about.

"What's going on in here?" he shouted, adding to chaos.

"A mouse! A mouse in the larder!" Eby screeched. She was up on the table in the center of the room, causing a grand stir.

Adelina didn't wait around long enough to hear the laird's undoubtedly cruel reply. She sprinted across the great hall, through the solar, and into Ronan's room. God bless Eby. Adelina certainly owed her more than boiled herbs.

"About time, Adelina. We've been waiting for you," Ronan said, looking askance at her as she leaned against the door to catch her breath.

Lucy, Lady Sybilla's maid, was sitting in a chair next to Ronan's bed.

Goosebumps ran up Adelina's arms. What was going on today? First Lady Sybilla, then Laird Calder. Now Lucy was behaving oddly.

Adelina must have looked confused. Lucy noticed first, offering an explanation.

"Lord Ronan asked me to come and speak with him about my lady," she said, her cheeks flushing with embarrassment.

"Oh," Adelina replied. Apparently she still wasn't going to get to check on Ronan's injuries. "I suppose I could step out," she offered. Then she remembered the raging laird. "There's only one problem," she began.

Lucy held up her hand, cutting her off. "There's no problem," she corrected gently. "'Tis not a matter of love I've come to speak of, but of betrayal."

A sinking feeling in the pit of her stomach told Adelina her day was about to get worse instead of better. "Betrayal?" she repeated.

"I summoned Lucy to inquire about Lady Sybilla's activities over the last few days," Ronan explained.

Adelina sighed. "You," she said, pointing a finger at Ronan, "are not to be doing anything as strenuous as questioning a maidservant while you recover from your injuries."

Ronan rolled his eyes. "While I would love nothing more than to lay infirm for days upon end, you and I both know more pressing matters are at hand. I will do what I must to aid my clan, even at risk of my own health."

"Fine," Adelina shot back, "but as your caretaker I strongly disapprove."

"And as my advisor?" Ronan asked.

Adelina fell into a chair beside Lucy. "I approve," she whispered in defeat.

"I don't mean to pry," Lucy said cautiously, "but mayhap I could give you more useful information if I knew what this was all about. Has Lady Sybilla done something wrong? Why are we speaking of betrayal?"

Adelina and Ronan exchanged a glance. "The less you know, the better," Ronan replied. "I simply wondered if you've noticed Lady Sybilla doing anything odd, or out of character. Particularly since you've arrived at Calder Keep."

"I should tell you," Lucy said after giving it some thought, "she's been behaving oddly, now that you mention it. She keeps asking about the fires they light for the Samhain festival. She sneaks away from me and wanders all over town on her own. I've no idea what she's doing or where she's going, and when I ask she never tells me anything about it. Oh," Lucy added, shifting to the edge of her seat, "yesterday after we left your room, lord, she spoke an awful lot of going to visit Adelina's cottage this morning. She was gone when I woke, but I thought it an odd comment."

The color drained from Adelina's face. In the pit of her stomach, she could feel Lady Sybilla's guilt. Perhaps she liked Adelina enough to spare her life, but not her belongings in her search for the letter. Or perhaps she was being selective about the use of violence, trying to make things look accidental when they did happen. But how had she known it was at Adelina's cottage?

"Is there anything else?" Lucy asked quietly. Tears were welling in her brown eyes. She must feel awful about betraying her mistress.

"I'm certain it wasn't easy to bring this forward," Ronan said gently. "You're free to go. And please, be discreet about this conversation. No one else need know for the time being."

"Aye," Lucy whispered. She fled quickly out the door, leaving roaring silence in her wake.

Admittedly, Adelina was rather happy to hear that Ronan likely wouldn't be marrying the treacherous Lady Sybilla. A host of new problems came along with this new piece of the puzzle, however. Not the first of which was Adelina's personal safety.

"My cottage was broken into last night," Adelina said. " And I saw her this morning, wandering around near my cottage."

"What! Why didn't you mention that sooner?" Ronan exclaimed.

"And have Lucy know even more than she already does? What good would that have done?"

"I don't know," Ronan said, calming at her logic, "But that seems important enough to tell me right away. Was the letter gone? Was anything else taken?"

Adelina shook her head. "Nothing was taken, and the letter is still safe. Several books were destroyed, though, including your library's copy of Cicero."

"The Devil take Cicero," Ronan grumbled. "I'm worried about you. We can get another copy. We cannot replace you."

Adelina snorted. "Your father might disagree with you there," she pointed out.

Ronan ignored her comment. "We should post a guard at your cottage."

Seconds after he finished his statement, his eyes brightened, and he swore roundly.

Adelina hadn't seen him so upset before. "What is it?" she asked.

"Guards," he replied, shaking his head at himself, "She asked me about the guards we were posting for Samhain."

"What!" Adelina shouted. "And it never occurred to you that was odd?" How had he not mentioned this sooner?

Ronan regarded her carefully before replying. "It did," he answered at last, "but I was distracted."

Adelina's stomach turned. She thought she might be sick. Had he been kissing Lady Sybilla? "Distracted?" she asked, unable to hide her concern.

"Lady Sybilla was riding next to me, but 'twas not Lady Sybilla I thought of while we rode," he explained. "I was so distracted thinking of you that she had to constantly call me back to our conversation. So you can understand," he said emphatically, "why perhaps I missed some details of it."

He had been thinking of her? The whole time he was out with Lady Sybilla? Mayhap he truly did care for her. "She could tell you were distracted?" Adelina pressed. She found she was suddenly much more interested in the details of his outing.

Ronan grinned wickedly. "Oh, aye," he fair laughed. "She could tell I was distracted, and she knew 'twas by you. She didn't hesitate to tell me as much."

"What did she say?" Adelina walked over to the foot of the bed, holding the post as she listened to his tale.

He suddenly looked uncomfortable, and hesitated in his reply.

"What is it?" she said, trying to prod him into answering.

"She said some very unladylike things," he admitted at last. "She was speaking rather forwardly about my relationship with you and my marriage to her."

It took Adelina a moment to divine exactly what he meant by that. Lady Sybilla must have had a frank conversation with him indeed.

"So you don't like it when women throw themselves at you?" she asked suggestively. Though she had no intention of doing any such thing, Adelina did enjoy teasing him.

"I don't like it when Lady Sybilla throws herself at me," Ronan corrected, sitting up in his bed. "There is a certain woman, however, who continues to elude my best efforts."

Adelina swallowed hard. She had intended a verbal game with him, but Ronan was entirely serious. His beautiful hazel eyes captured her gaze with devastating sincerity. Adelina knew she was in danger now.

Chapter Nineteen

Adelina suddenly felt quite a bit like throwing herself at Ronan. She took a step back from the bed, reluctantly putting distance between them. She dare not speak, for fear of giving away just how much she wanted to run to him.

Ronan pressed onward, unrelenting in his speech. Now that he had begun telling her how he truly felt, he showed no sign of stopping. "I keep thinking back to the other night," he whispered. "The awful one, when the missive came."

"Why?" Adelina squeaked out. Why would he ever think about that? 'Twas a wretched event.

"So many things about that night made me angry," he replied, the memory clearly in his sight once more, "So many important things happened. And yet, all I can remember is the way the fading firelight danced in your hair. Gold and orange glowing against the red. Like a sunset."

Her heart pounded, hardly contained in her chest. No one had ever spoken like that to her before. And still, he kept going.

"I see the outline of you," his eyes clouded with emotion as he spoke, "barely hidden under a thin nightgown, waiting to be touched. And I will never forget how you looked that night wearing my plaid, like a true Highland lass. Like my lass."

Before she could think about what she was doing, Adelina unwrapped his plaid from about her shoulders. She did it slowly, deliberately, looking right into his gorgeous eyes. Then her hands went to the laces on her gown.

At first he looked sad. She knew he didn't like that she was taking off his plaid. But as she continued, first confusion and then desire took hold of his face.

She unlaced the bodice of the gown, hoping she didn't look ridiculous. She'd heard one of her brother's friends tell a story once, a very naughty one, and the fact that the woman had undressed for the man had always stuck with her. If she was going to throw herself at a man, that seemed the best way to do it.

Ronan moved like he was going to get out of bed, and Adelina stopped abruptly. He was instantly crestfallen.

"I will only continue," she said in the most seductive tone she could muster, "if you remain seated."

A wicked grin lit up his face, and he leaned back against his bed once more.

Adelina's fingers trembled. She wet her lips with her tongue, then pressed onward. Based upon his reaction she must not look terribly ridiculous, at least.

Even unlaced, her overdress was a bit fitted. She had to wiggle it over her hips before it fell to the floor. Ronan shifted on the bed, but stayed put.

She did a leisurely spin, lifting her arms to her head so that he could see the outline of her beneath her chemise. Just as he remembered from the night of the meeting. She had worn her hair down every day since then, knowing how much he liked it. It trailed behind her like a cloak of fire.

When she had made a full turn, Adelina tugged the chemise over her shoulders. When it came loose over her arms, she let it fall in a puddle atop her dress. She became acutely aware that she was now completely naked in front of Ronan.

Fighting mortification, she forced herself to look up at him. She worried he might be disgusted or uninterested. Mayhap amused. His jaw was tight, his breathing shallow. She could tell that even from across the room. His hazel eyes drank in every inch of her, top to bottom. He didn't look about to laugh at her. Nay, he looked like he might devour her.

Adelina was suddenly at a loss for what happened next. "What should I do?" she asked him, unable to keep from blushing at her own boldness.

"Come here," he ordered. His voice was low, filled with emotion.

She tiptoed over to him, her feet chilled on the stone floor. When she came within arms' reach of him, he grabbed hold of her hips and pulled her onto his lap so that she faced him. His warm hands caressed her bare skin, running over every inch of her.

"I'll do whatever you tell me," she whispered, "as long as you don't move."

He raised an eyebrow at that order.

"You shouldn't overexert yourself," she explained, his busy hands nearly driving her to distraction, "maybe you can walk and move about, but you shouldn't do anything strenuous."

He kissed her shoulder, his breath hot on her cold skin. "What is it you want, lass?" he asked her.

"I want to be with you." 'Twas the most honest answer she could think of.

His lips moved lower, grazing the top of her breast. She was having more and more difficulty continuing the conversation.

"Do you know what that means?" he asked playfully. There wasn't a hint of condescension in his tone, only curiosity. And quite a bit of lust.

She licked her lips. "In theory," she answered, "but not really in practice. You'll have to tell me what to do."

He paused in his kisses, grasping her face lovingly between his hands. He kissed her softly, sweetly. When he pulled away his hands went to her breasts. She inhaled, arching her back as he massaged her.

"Touch me," he directed her, "like I am touching you."

She ran her hands over his tight, muscled chest. Her fingers encircled his strong arms and she marveled at his masculine perfection. Ronan watched as her eyes roamed his torso. Then something a bit lower caught her eye.

Ronan brought his lips to hers, kissing her with the full force of his need. His fingers moved across her body, touching, exploring, driving her to madness with desire. While they kissed, Adelina worked up the courage to move aside Ronan's blankets. She gently ran her hands over him.

He groaned in pleasure, and that was all the encouragement she needed. Carefully working her hands beneath his trousers, she began rubbing him, fascinated by how hard he was. His breathing grew ragged, and his fingers made their way between her legs. It felt so good when he massaged her there.

"Lift yourself up, lass," he breathed into her neck as he bathed her in wet kisses.

She rose up onto her knees, her breasts now right in front of his face. He grinned up at her before taking one of her hard nipples into his mouth. At the same time, he grabbed her hips and pulled her over his hard length, guiding her down until he was deep inside her.

Adelina gasped in pleasure. For the briefest moment she felt some discomfort, but when she moved her hips it went away. Ronan groaned again, and a fire rose up within her. She needed something, desperately.

She could feel it like an emptiness within her. Yet she could not put a name to it.

"Move your hips, lass," he urged her, helping her rock atop him, grasping her hips. It took several attempts, but soon she had the motion of it. As she grew more confident, she moved faster and faster, until both were gasping for breath.

Heat swelled up from where they were joined, pushing her closer and closer so something she couldn't quite reach. Adelina moaned, throwing her head back and lifting herself even more as she rode him.

His breath caught, and she felt him harden inside of her. He grabbed her, pulling her down while also pushing himself harder into her. She squeezed him right back, until she thought she couldn't take the pleasure of it any longer. The heat, the pressure, the passion built up into a spiraling crescendo.

Then the world went dark for a moment. Adelina lost all track of her surroundings, and felt like she might be falling. She cried out for Ronan, reaching for him and pulling herself into him. He held her right back, and she could tell from his expression that he had experienced something just the same. He ran his hands through her hair; kissed her forehead. Together they collapsed onto the soft bed, smiling.

Chapter Twenty

Adelina was amazing. Ronan basked in the feel of her snuggled against him. Laying her head on his chest, he could just see her face below his shoulder. She was warm and soft and feminine. He rested his chin on the top of her head, taking in the sweet scent of lavender. He could do this every day for the rest of his life.

Her eyes moved back and forth, with increasing speed. They were the most enchanting shade of blue, one he'd never seen before. They complemented her ivory skin and brilliant red hair perfectly. Blue like the shallows of the loch, reflecting the sun. Aye, that's what they reminded him of.

"What are you thinking about?" he asked, watching her with contentment. She was always thinking, always planning. That much he knew from the day they had met.

When she tilted her head toward him, he could see more clearly her distress. "I just remembered that I came here today to check in on you." She sounded horrified that she hadn't accomplished her mission.

"Allow me to assist you, my lady," he offered in his most chivalrous tone.

Adelina giggled, a sound that sent joy straight to his heart. She sat up, like a cat waking from an afternoon nap. Lord, she was still naked.

Ronan felt himself getting aroused all over again. He had as much self-control as a young lad, apparently. It wasn't his fault she was so beautiful. He ran his hands over her stomach playfully as she walked on her knees to sit behind him. She kissed his cheek, but he could tell she meant business.

Her hands unwrapped the bandage she had put on his head the day before, brushing aside his hair so that she could get a better look.

"How does it look?" he asked, only mildly curious.

"Like you smacked your head on a log," she retorted.

He couldn't help but laugh. When she was happy, her joy was infectious. By God, he was happy, too. That realization hit him harder than any log had. Ronan felt happy for the first time in years.

He couldn't explain it, but as she worked to re-bandage his wound, he desperately wanted an even deeper connection with her. The irrepressible urge to bring her into his life in a meaningful way filled him with the courage to say something he had *never* said before.

"Ask me something," the words felt foreign on his lips, "I'll tell you anything."

She didn't do him the dishonor of questioning his intentions. Instead, she finished up what she was doing and moved to sit in front of him, in all her glorious nudity. She thought for a long minute before asking her chosen query.

"Why is there no lady of the keep? There are hardly any women at all here," she said.

Ronan sighed deeply, but felt somehow like this was the right time to tell her his deepest, darkest secret.

"'Tis a long, sad tale, lass," he began, preparing her for what was to come.

She moved back to sit behind him again, this time massaging his shoulders. "I want to know, and I want to help," she whispered.

He swelled with pride in the woman he had chosen to love. She was never afraid to learn the truth of something, and she was always, *always* ready to be there for him.

He told her the tale that had haunted his clan for two generations. "Many years ago we had a fine healer in Clan Calder. One winter, when she was getting on in years, she succumbed to an ague. We have not had a proper healer since. A few have come. Some were good, others left. Not long after she died, a rumor started that our clan was cursed. I've no idea how or why, but it stuck.

"Without a skilled healer, we lose many who ought to live. In particular, we lose women to childbirth. A few have lived through all their children's births. I've no idea if 'tis the usual amount of women who die in such a manner, or if we lose many more than we ought.

"There is no lady of the house," he began, but his voice failed him.

Adelina wrapped her arms around him, supporting him.

"There is no lady of the house," he tried again, this time with more control, "because my mother, and not long after my only sister, died the same way. 'Tis the truth I've refused to take a wife for fear she'd die birthing my child."

She laid her head on his shoulder, a river of fiery curls falling down his chest. "Ronan, I'm so sorry," she said softly.

"I haven't spoken to anyone except Brother Gilbert of it," he said, "Though as a lad I did try to speak with my father."

"I don't imagine that went particularly well," Adelina surmised.

Ronan scoffed softly. Adelina had only ever seen the worst of his father. "He used to be kinder," Ronan offered. "When I was a boy, he'd play with me. He doted on my sister. When my mother passed, he was distant. When my sister died, he was gone. He's never been the same man since."

"How long ago was this?" Adelina asked, as though there were hope that the laird might come around.

"My niece will be seven soon," Ronan said wistfully. "I still need to decide what to send her."

Adelina shot around to sit in front of him again. "You have a niece!" she said excitedly, "And you send her birthday gifts?"

"Yes, I have a niece," Ronan said defensively, "And of course I send her gifts. I write her letters several times a year as well. My father is happier ignoring her existence." He could forgive the man his grief over wife and daughter, but there was no need to ignore the people he still had in his life.

"Your father is deeply wounded by his losses," Adelina observed, "It only makes sense he wouldn't want to face them, in any form."

Ronan relaxed. He nodded in agreement, content that he was not alone in his concerns. He saw Adelina's mind racing once more, and he knew she'd have something insightful to add. He waited while she sorted it out.

"You know," she started, "I have a good friend who is a master healer. I'm certain if you needed her, she would come."

"I thought you were a healer," Ronan replied. Wasn't she healing him right now? He knew she'd been seeing villagers and offering cures for all manner of ailments.

"I was studying under her," Adelina explained, "I know enough to be helpful. But her knowledge is far beyond anything I could hope to achieve. For Gemma, healing is like breathing."

"She is English?" Ronan asked with distaste. Though he quite enjoyed Adelina's company, there were already two Englishwomen living on Calder lands. One of whom was plotting to murder his father. 'Twould be difficult to convince Laird Calder and the elders to allow yet another Englishwoman to visit.

Adelina shoved him with a laugh. "Aye, she is English."

"I doubt my father would allow it, in that case," Ronan said.

A bolt of worry flickered across Adelina's delicate features, as though she remembered something terribly important. "Your father!" she repeated.

"What of him?" Ronan asked. He had a feeling he wouldn't like where this was going.

"I'm not supposed to be here," Adelina said, "He stopped me from coming into the keep this morning. He thinks *I'm* the traitor!"

Dread settled about Ronan like an old friend. He'd have to deal with his father soon. He couldn't let Adelina be tormented any longer. For now, he wanted only the quiet afternoon they shared.

He ran his hands through her hair, down her silken arms, until they rested atop her own. Her worry coursed through her as clearly as the sun crossed the sky at midday.

"'Twill be alright, lass," he soothed, pulling her against his chest and hugging her. "Stay here with me. We'll lie abed, have supper brought, and worry over my father in the morn. For what is left of this day, let there be only us."

Adelina looked up at him with her liquid blue eyes, filled with fear and hope. And love. How had he lived without her before? How would he live without her ever? Ronan pushed his troublesome thoughts to the back of his mind. He wanted only Adelina, only this moment. Soon enough, he would face the daylight.

For now, theirs was the night.

Chapter Twenty-One

October 27, 1136

Ronan!" Adelina chided him. A profusion of giggles followed her reprimand.

He was utterly unrepentant. He continued kissing her neck as she struggled leaf through the pages of Donatus. It would seem that her neck was quite ticklish.

Ronan couldn't bear to let her leave that morning. The thought of continuing his day without her filled him with emptiness. Instead, he had accompanied her back to the library. He acted a perfect gentleman while they made their way through town. Once they arrived inside the cozy building, however, Ronan had other ideas.

She turned around and kissed him square on his mouth. Her sweet taste consumed his senses once more, and he brought his hands to her hips. When he drew her closer, she smacked his hands playfully and broke the kiss.

"*You*," she accused him, "are a distraction."

"Aye, lass," he agreed, "'Tis the idea." He rubbed her shoulders, only occasionally allowing his hands to squeeze other parts as well. She giggled every time he strayed.

Adelina turned back to the letter before her. "I have to get this done, or we'll be in trouble."

"I leave you two alone for, what, a week? And now you're hanging off her like a cloak," a stern voice shouted from the door.

They both turned and watched Brother Gilbert remove his own cloak, a broad smile across his weathered face.

Ronan felt a great weight lift from him. Brother Gilbert had returned, giving them another ally in their battle against the traitorous Lady Sybilla. He looked relieved to be home. "You've been missed, friend," Ronan greeted him.

Brother Gilbert rolled his eyes heavenward. "Well you could have fooled me," he said wryly. He raised his eyebrows, taking in Ronan's hands on Adelina's shoulders.

"We've been counting the days till you returned to us," Adelina added. Ronan saw deep relief in her eyes as well. Brother Gilbert was full of both reason and wisdom, something much needed around Calder Keep these days.

"I am glad to be back, though 'tis the truth I must leave again on the morrow. Apparently my services are in high demand now that I'm to be heading back to the monastery soon," Brother Gilbert said sadly.

"Surely there must be other priests in the Highlands?" Adelina asked, closing the book before her.

"None as fine as our Brother Gilbert," Ronan replied. He knew how lucky they were to have such a good man amongst them for so long.

Brother Gilbert waved a hand, as though swatting away the compliment. He sank into his chair and sighed. "I wasn't even a priest to begin with, lass," he explained. "I left my monastery to come and advise Clan Calder. When I arrived, I realized there wasn't a man of God to be found. My superiors gave me permission to be ordained to perform priestly sacraments, that I might fill the great gap in services here."

Adelina frowned. “Then who will take over such duties when you leave us?”

Ronan swelled with pride. She considered herself one of the clan already.

“I’ve been speaking with your cousin,” Brother Gilbert said, nodding toward Ronan, “Colban. I think he holds great promise as a man of the cloth.”

Ronan nodded. He couldn’t agree more. The lad certainly wasn’t a warrior, that much he knew.

“Before I forget,” Brother Gilbert said, jumping to his feet and pulling a letter from his robes, “Beatrix sends her regards.”

“How is she?” Ronan asked, suddenly overcome with concern for his niece. He should have thought to send her gift with Brother Gilbert. Hopefully she wasn’t terribly disappointed.

“No need to fret,” Brother Gilbert assured him, “she’s growing into a wonderful young lass. Her looks favor her mother, but she has all the ambition of her father.”

Ronan’s heart warmed. He dearly loved hearing about his niece, though he was shamefully bad at visiting her in person. In truth, the thought of seeing her pained him. He feared it would sour his feelings toward her, to see his sister’s image in another. ‘Twas no time to dwell on such ridiculous notions now.

“Brother Gilbert,” Adelina began tentatively, “I believe we require your assistance.”

“Oh?” Brother Gilbert replied.

“We received a letter from Aidan,” Ronan explained, “And we can’t read the last line.”

“Aidan!” Brother Gilbert said with shock. “Where is he? How is he?”

Ronan shook his head. If only he knew. “All we know is that he signed the letter, and ‘tis confusing enough that he was almost certainly the author.”

Brother Gilbert grinned, a picture of joy. Ronan understood exactly how he felt. Everyone in the family had believed Aidan dead. The letter meant there was yet hope of finding him. "Let me see the letter," he offered.

Adelina handed it to him, and he read it aloud.

"*Inve nicar duumet sic am. Pro dit orest*," he intoned. "But that makes no sense. It's incomprehensible."

"Which is exactly why we need your help," Adelina said.

Before Brother Gilbert could respond, a lad appeared in the doorway, no more than fifteen, shuffling his feet back and forth.

"What can we help you with, lad?" Brother Gilbert asked kindly.

"My ma," he replied, "she sent me to fetch the healer."

Adelina's back straightened, and she jumped right in. "What's the trouble?" she asked.

The boy looked about the room, as though he hadn't expected to speak with anyone other than Adelina.

"I need to know what supplies I'll be needing," Adelina added.

"My wee sister," he answered finally, "She won't stop coughing. Ma's going mad with worry. She's near to tears whenever the fits come on." His voice cracked as he spoke.

Adelina had started packing supplies before the lad had finished his explanation. Earlier that morning, Ronan had helped her move what was left of her herbs and tonics to the library to keep them safe. She grabbed her cloak and brushed past the lad on her way out the door. The boy followed, hot on her heels.

Worry descended on Ronan as he watched her head to the stables. Lady Sybilla could plan to target Adelina just as easily as she had him. He couldn't let anything happen to her.

"I'm going with you," he declared, saddling his destrier.

A bright smile formed on Adelina's beautiful face. "Wonderful," she replied, mounting her own horse.

Fingal, as Ronan learned the lad's name was, led them on a two-hour trip to the easternmost settlement. He stopped at a small cottage in a sorry state of disrepair. Ronan would mention to his father that many of the cottages in this settlement needed attention. Perhaps before the snows came some of these roofs could be repaired.

They heard the wee babe coughing before they had dismounted. Adelina threw herself from her horse, grabbing her satchel and rushing inside. Ronan and Fingal tied up the horses and followed her into the crowded room.

"She's coughing so much 'tis making her sick," Fingal's mother cried. She rocked the baby desperately while the child kept coughing.

"Hold her up, and we'll get this tonic in her," Adelina instructed, pulling a stoppered jar from her satchel.

She held something beneath the babe's tiny nose, strong enough to stop her cough so they could pour the liquid in her mouth. The babe sputtered and spit, but it was clear some of the tonic made its way down.

Adelina spent a long moment watching the mother fretting over her tiny daughter. Then she pulled another jar from her bag.

"This one is for you," she said, offering it to the mother.

"Me?" the woman looked shocked by the suggestion.

Adelina nodded, thrusting the jar into the woman's hands and taking the infant. "'Tis no easy task, managing a sick child alone. The tonic will give you strength while the babe heals."

The woman looked instantly relieved. She drank from the jar, then put it back in the satchel. Adelina insisted that the woman go out for a walk and get some fresh air while she and Ronan watch the babe. She explained that it was necessary for the tonic to work, and that it would give her time to ensure the babe was improving.

Ronan went outside to start patching the roof. He might as well do something useful if they were to spend the afternoon here. He sent Fingal to collect straw so they could add more thatching.

Adelina brought the babe out to watch, and had her crawling around on the soft grass. She cooed and sang to the child, talking softly and tickling the little one's toes. Every so often she would cradle the babe in her arms and pat her back.

As Ronan watched Adelina with the child, a flood of emotions swept through him. When first he saw them together, Ronan was enchanted. Adelina made it look so easy, so joyful. He hadn't spent any time around a babe, but he knew enough of the difficulty of raising them from what little he'd seen around the keep. Watching them, he forgot everything but the beauty of such a bond.

'Twasn't long, however, before the panic set in. It began when Ronan thought of Adelina playing with his child. A natural progression, given the situation. But what if she were pregnant already?

Lord, why had he slept with her? Why hadn't he realized that in just one night he had put the only woman he'd ever fallen in love with at risk of death? Good God, if she were already with child he could lose her within a year. He was dumbfounded. How could he be so stupid, so selfish?

Ronan had no idea how he would continue courting her. He couldn't. That was what it amounted to. If he cared for her at all, he couldn't continue putting her at risk for his own pleasure. He wasn't certain what to do next, but he knew he absolutely could not take her to his bed again.

They spent the next few hours helping Fingal and his mother, Brigit, fix up the one-room cottage. Adelina helped with the babe while Brigit cleaned, swept, and cooked. Ronan taught Fingal how to patch the roof, and they made a good start on it. Brigit begged them to stay for supper, but Ronan insisted they return to the keep before dusk. She sent them home with honey cake instead.

Ronan helped Adelina mount her horse but made certain his hands didn't linger anywhere this time. She said her good-byes as he mounted

Sólas, making sweet faces at the baby as he spurred his destrier into motion. Adelina had to hurry her mare along to catch up.

"Are you alright?" she asked when she finally closed the gap between them.

Ronan was far from alright, but he wasn't about to plague Adelina with his troubles. She had done a good thing today, and he wouldn't take that from her.

"Just excited to get back," he muttered.

"Are you dreading telling your father about Lady Sybilla?"

Ronan sighed, knowing she wouldn't like his answer. "I would like another day to think on the matter before speaking with the laird. I don't want to be rashly accusing a noblewoman of so serious a crime."

Adelina looked at him skeptically, but said nothing.

Ronan kept his own counsel for the ride, trying to sort out the conflicting emotions which threatened to take over all reason. After two hours, he still didn't know how he could ever give Adelina up.

Chapter Twenty-Two

October 29, 1136

Adelina was, quite literally, out of thyme. She'd collected quite a few strange looks as she walked through the village staring at the ground. Likely it had less to do with her wandering and more to do with the scowl she knew she wore. Something was wrong with Ronan, something relating to her, and for whatever reason he wasn't visiting her.

Two days ago they had rode out with Fingal to help his wee sister. At some point from when they left Calder village to when they returned, Ronan had changed. That morning he couldn't keep his hands off her. When they returned to the stables that evening he couldn't get away from her fast enough.

Of course, she was likely overreacting. Mayhap he remembered something important, and it had nothing to do at all with Adelina. 'Tis the truth that a great flaw of hers was thinking she was at the center of everyone's problems.

Dismissing her selfish concerns, Adelina threw on Ronan's plaid and grabbed her largest basket. She packed a small loaf of bread and two apples, then headed out her door. Even though she knew she was being ridiculous, she couldn't quite shake the feeling of worry from her thoughts.

The Highlands in autumn were a sight to behold. Shades of purple, yellow, and orange blended with greens and browns as the weather took a turn toward winter. Sweeps of color wound up and down the hillsides, reaching their peaks around a loch in the distance. A few pine trees stood proudly towering over the fading greenery.

Adelina walked for a good hour before she reached the loch. She could have ridden, of course, but after sitting in the library for hours beyond count, her legs demanded the exercise. The cold was so pervasive that she could taste the chill in the air with every breath. She collapsed onto a frigid grey stone along the shore of the loch, an icy wind blowing in to greet her. In a few moments she had regained her strength, and stood to begin her search for the elusive herb.

As she wandered the rocky shore, Adelina couldn't keep Ronan from her mind. Yesterday he had been to the library, she told herself optimistically. But, she recalled, he'd mostly spoken with Brother Gilbert, who was on his way out. Ronan hadn't even hugged her before he'd retreated to the keep.

Today he'd not come at all. Her heart was heavy with that realization. Mayhap he'd come later and she'd just missed him while she was out. Or mayhap he'd remembered that she was nothing but a commoner and thought better of taking her to bed. He could run back to Lady Sybilla and make a match of standing.

She shook such nonsense from her mind. Of course he couldn't marry Lady Sybilla. She was a criminal plotting to murder his father.

Relief washed over Adelina when her eyes caught sight of a plant with purple flowers and tiny triangular leaves. Thyme. She knelt and began collecting enough for the next couple of weeks, careful to leave plenty of flowers to reseed and enough leaves to keep the plants healthy.

Adelina heard the hoof beats first.

Panic shot through her. Had Lady Sybilla followed her here? She hadn't thought of that when she'd set out. She knew there was no point in hiding. The rider would've seen her over a crest long before she heard the horse coming.

Shielding her eyes from the sun's glare, she searched the horizon for the incoming rider. Instantly, she recognized the horse. Sólas. And glaring at her from his destrier's back was Ronan. Lord, but he looked angry.

"What exactly do you think you're doing?" he shouted, jumping down from his mount before the horse had even stopped. His beautiful hazel eyes narrowed at her accusingly.

Adelina backed away from him, the force of his anger taking her by surprise. What on earth had she done to make him so mad? "I'm collecting herbs," she explained, "There wasn't any more thyme in the village, so..."

He cut her off. "So you thought you'd walk over an hour away, alone, without telling anyone you were leaving?"

Ah, so that was it. He was worried about her. She tried to soothe him, but he just kept yelling at her.

"Don't you realize that someone could have followed you? Anything could have happened. You should always have someone with you outside the village until all this business with the traitor gets sorted," he bellowed, the muscles in his jaw so tight she thought it might burst.

Her own rage rose like the tide, in answer to his rudeness. All sympathy for his concern dissipated.

"Well," she retorted, hands on her hips, "if *someone* had been around, I wouldn't have been out here alone."

"It may shock you, but I do have duties other than minding you," he offered as an explanation.

"Minding me?" she seethed, "Is that what you're calling it? Lucky for you I no longer need to be 'minded'. As well you can see, I am a grown woman and perfectly capable of going out on my own. Without you."

He threw his hands in the air, as though her statement was utterly ridiculous. "I know that if a man intending to hurt you rode out instead of me, you'd be dead by now."

She chose to overlook the fact that she herself had that very same thought only moments ago. Instead, she focused on how little she cared for him ordering her around.

"How dare you ride all the way out here, just to yell at me for doing my job!" she shouted, motioning to her basket of thyme.

In two steps he closed the distance between them, his face inches from hers.

"If you were doing your job," he hissed, "you'd be back at the keep advising my father about the clan."

She had the urge to kiss him and slap him all at the same time. "If you'll recall," she reminded him tartly, "I'm not allowed to set foot in the keep. Let alone offer your father my advice."

He took a step back, and she knew she'd struck a chord. She pressed her advantage.

"Why haven't you spoken to him on my behalf?" she questioned angrily. "Why haven't you had Lady Sybilla arrested to protect the clan?"

"Why are you out here on your own, risking your life for no good reason? Why aren't you working to read the letter?" he countered, his voice softer.

Adelina relented. She was still furious at him provoking her for no reason, but if he wasn't going to shout neither would she. "I needed some fresh air," she said, throwing her hands up. "I'll go right back to my work when I return to the library, have no worry over that. Unlike you, I take this letter, and Lady Sybilla's threat to the clan, seriously."

Ronan sighed deeply, running his hands through his dark hair. "That's what I came to speak with you about, actually," he said, his voice calmer.

"Lady Sybilla?" Adelina asked, alarmed.

"The library," Ronan clarified.

"What of it?" Adelina bristled. "I'm still talking about Lady Sybilla. I thought once we agreed the evidence was damning, we'd have her locked up and be done with it."

"'Tis more complicated than that," Ronan said, his voice pained.

Like hell it was more complicated. Mayhap Ronan was still interested in Lady Sybilla, and refused to believe her guilt because of his affection.

Adelina strode right up to him, jabbing his muscular chest with her index finger to make sure he heard her. "Samhain Eve is tomorrow, Ronan," she reminded him, "We don't have time to mess around with 'complicated'. If we don't do something, your father could be murdered and your clan destroyed."

He took hold of her finger gently, giving her hand a squeeze. "We can talk about that more later," he conceded. "I came here looking for you. To make sure you were safe."

"What do you mean?"

Ronan swallowed hard. "The library was torn apart. Someone is still looking for the letter, and they know you have it. Whatever is in that last line is making the traitor more desperate, to do something so obvious."

That was all Ronan had to say. Adelina hurried to grab her basket of thyme, their argument all but forgotten. She waited for him to lift her up in front of him atop Sólas. Then her strong warrior spurred the black destrier, wrapping his arms about her as they rode.

Adelina was wracked with worry over her own safety, over Lady Sybilla's plotting, over Ronan's cold behavior. The only comfort she took was in the warmth of Ronan's embrace, and even that couldn't keep away all of the autumn's chill.

Chapter Twenty-Three

Everything was destroyed. The ruins of decades of work, Brother Gilbert's legacy, lay in jagged heaps of lost knowledge. Adelina crumpled to the ground alongside the devastation.

Ronan stood behind her, close enough that she could feel his presence though not quite touching her.

She felt tears welling, and covered her face with her hands. Brother Gilbert would be beside himself. He had believed in her, as had Ronan. When she came to Calder, it had been a thriving Highland village. In less than a fortnight, she had fallen out of favor with the laird, unable to help him with the clan's most pressing issue, and seen the greatest collection of manuscripts in the Highlands reduced to shreds.

Ronan said nothing. Instead, he began collecting the scraps of parchment and vellum, placing them in neat stacks on the table.

Adelina watched him, peeking from behind her hand so she only need gaze at a small slice of the chaos surrounding her.

"If you can manage it," he said, continuing to pick up the pieces of the library, "'twould help for you to see what's salvageable of these."

Taking a deep breath, Adelina slowly rose to her feet and made her way over to the table. The books she had been reading when she needed a break from deciphering the letter had been treated the most brutally. Many of the pages Ronan had collected belonged to the two herbals she had been studying to improve her healing skills. She picked up a page from the other book she had found tucked away in the library's shelves. She'd been so excited when she found it, for she had never seen anything like it before.

"What's that?" Ronan asked, bringing another stack of pages to the table and looking over her shoulder at the paper in her hand.

"It's an aqueduct," Adelina answered. "The Romans used them to distribute water throughout cities."

Ronan nodded, looking at the pages on the table with greater interest. He picked up a few and looked at the multitude of fascinating machines and buildings drawn in painstaking detail. "This looks just the same as the stained-glass window in the great hall," Ronan commented, pointing to a drawing of a keystone arch.

"Aye," Adelina agreed. "They can bear more weight with that design."

"I didn't realize 'twas a Roman one," Ronan said with a chuckle.

A noise near the door drew their attention. "God's bones! Lucy said the library was in tatters, but I thought for certain she was exaggerating," Lady Sybilla exclaimed, gliding swiftly into the room.

Adelina charged straight for her, uncontrollable fury driving all reason from her. "How dare you come here!" she shouted.

"Lord, Adelina, I know you're upset, but that's really no way to greet a friendly face," Lady Sybilla chided her.

"How can you pretend any longer?" Adelina questioned, "How can you claim to be my friend and then turn around and destroy the library? Break into my cottage in the middle of the night? Just admit that you're the traitor already!"

"Adelina," Ronan interrupted, coming over to stand between the two women, "that's no way to speak to Lady Sybilla, traitor or no."

Lady Sybilla stared at them both. "Traitor?" she repeated. "What on earth are you talking about? You think I did this?"

"Well didn't you?" Adelina shot back. "I know you've been tearing apart my things to find that letter. And what about when you asked Ronan about guards being posted on Samhain? Are you saying you're not plotting something?"

Lady Sybilla held up one hand, palm facing Adelina, to stop her tirade. "Now just a moment," she said tightly, pushing past Ronan to get closer to Adelina, "I have no idea what traitor or letter it is you speak of, but I do know this. I have watched as you throw yourself at my future husband. I have stood by, and let your little romance continue because I thought you harmless." She lowered her mouth to Adelina's ear so that Ronan could no longer overhear their conversation.

"Don't think for one moment that pointing some imaginary finger at me will stop my marrying Ronan," she whispered venomously, "I am plotting something, little scholar. I am plotting to have Ronan all to myself on Samhain night. And while I enjoy a bit of excitement, I'd prefer not having any guards around when I finally make him mine. If I no longer think you harmless, I will have to take action." She turned away from Adelina without another glance, giving Ronan's shoulder a squeeze as she walked to the door. "I'll see you at supper, dear," she said, vanishing back into the village.

"Can you believe her?" Adelina cried, gesturing angrily at the empty doorway.

Ronan turned a dark look at her. "That was improper."

"I know!" Adelina agreed. "That's what I mean. How dare she be so bold?"

He shook his head, his bright hazel eyes staring her down. "Not Sybilla," he corrected her, "You."

"Me?"

"Yes, you," Ronan folded his arms across his broad chest. "You shouldn't have accused her so openly, and certainly not with such anger."

"Why not?" Adelina countered, "Because she's a noblewoman?"

Ronan threw up his hands with a sigh. "Yes, Adelina, because she's a noblewoman. Even I wouldn't have addressed her thusly."

Adelina drew her lips into a thin line. She wanted to scream. She wanted to shout. But mostly she wanted to cry. "Get out," was all she managed.

"I'm not trying to upset you," he said softly. "I know you are worried over many things."

A single tear slipped down her cheek. He wiped it away, his thumb gently rubbing her cold skin.

"Why don't you want me anymore?" she whispered her question, afraid of his answer.

Ronan sighed yet again but didn't turn away from her. "Tomorrow morn, I'll come find you. There's a few more bonfires yet to build. You can help me with them, and you can have that explanation you're wanting," he replied.

"Why not tonight?" she pleaded. She didn't want to hold onto her anger, her frustration, her anxiety until the morning. Lord, how would she sleep?

"Just give it one more night, *mo cridhe*," he said softly, brushing her hair away from her face. With that, he slipped into the fading afternoon light.

Adelina sat at the table, staring at the mess her life had become. She knew she should set to work picking up the pieces, but she no longer had the heart to continue on alone. Instead, Adelina wandered down the village lanes, slowly making her way to her cottage and trying not to think of what tomorrow might bring.

CHAPTER TWENTY-FOUR

Samhain Eve – October 30, 1136

The rough timbers were testing the strength of his grasp. Oh, he'd carried cabers all his life. Some bigger than others. This morn, of course, he had picked up the three largest timbers awaiting the bonfire. He was paying for it now, hauling them up the steep hill. He endured this silent struggle while Adelina carried a bundle of sticks uphill beside him, waiting impatiently for him to offer her an explanation for his behavior. Anger emanated from her like steam, filling the space between them.

The trick of it was that he had nothing to say. He'd thought all night. Aye, he hadn't slept a wink. And still no words came. He couldn't bear to tell her he was finished with her. What sort of monster would she think him? To use a woman in his bed once and be done with her.

And yet he could hardly tell her the truth of it, that he was so damn scared for her life that he couldn't risk the possibility of getting her with child. If she believed him, she'd surely try to convince him 'twas a foolish fear. And at the end of it she'd still think he had no good reason at all for ending their intimacy.

Thus Ronan came once more full circle in his thoughts, still unable to choose the right words to tell her what he was feeling. 'Twas not something he did often in the first place. And these were particularly deep and troublesome feelings.

So he said nothing at all.

He could all but hear her grumbling over his reticence. Each step up the hill her frustration gained traction. Still, he knew no words that would fix it. Still, he said nothing.

When at long last they crested the hill, Adelina threw her bundle of sticks to the ground so that her hands were free to gesticulate her anger. First, they went straight to her hips. Aggressively.

He set down his cabers, bracing himself for the onslaught.

"So?" she prompted him.

"So what?" he asked, knowing full well it didn't sound as well-meaning as he'd intended.

"Take your pick," she retorted, "Why haven't you told your father of Lady Sybilla's guilt? Why have you been avoiding me at every turn?"

"Let's start with us," Ronan replied, his voice far calmer than his pounding heart.

"Oh," Adelina interjected, jumping on his words, "Is there an 'us'? Because from what I can tell, you flirted me into bed for a night and then tossed me aside."

Ronan began piling the cabers against the pyre that was already being built. What could he say to that? She wasn't wrong. "I know it seems that way," he started, "but the truth is just the opposite."

"Please," she said scathingly, "explain it to me."

What could he tell her but the truth? "If I get you with child, you would die," he answered.

Her face softened, and she gazed at him a long moment. "Is that truly it?" she asked.

"Of course that's it," he said.

"Not every woman dies in childbirth, Ronan. I know you've had some terrible experiences with it, but I know many women who have survived."

"Did your mother survive it?" he asked.

Adelina hesitated. "Well, actually, she didn't, but she was quite a bit older. It was more difficult for her."

"I see." And Ronan saw alright. He could see that she would never accept his reasoning, and she would never believe 'twas the only thing keeping him from her.

"I'll tell you what," she offered, her face brightening with her idea, "if ever that should happen, I'll invite Gemma to come stay with us. She's a wonderfully skilled healer. I'd be in the best hands."

Ronan sighed in exasperation. "'Tis not enough," he replied sadly.

The brightness faded from her beautiful face, replaced by fiery anger. "Fine," she conceded. "Let's talk about Lady Sybilla, then."

"I think we need more evidence," he explained. 'Twas the truth. They had hardly done a thorough investigation, even after they spoke with Lucy. 'Twould be fair to say Ronan had been a bit distracted lately, and hadn't paid the letter the attention it deserved.

Adelina's hands swung about wildly in exasperation. "More evidence?"

Ronan thought the tone of her voice was a bit much given what he'd said. He could tell he was heading for trouble again. "Aye," he confirmed, "more evidence. More than the word of a lady's maid and our own conjecture."

Her eyes narrowed dangerously. Damn, though, she was beautiful when she was riled. He only wished her anger weren't directed at him. He'd love to watch someone else take hell from her. "She helped to throw you from your horse!"

"We've no proof of it," Ronan countered, trying not to get worked up along with her. "I simply feel that we're rushing into an accusation that holds a great deal of weight."

"Rushing?" Adelina was livid. Her face was nearly as red as her hair, and she had started storming about the hilltop. "*Rushing?* We have waited, so far, until literally the last possible day to act. That's the opposite of rushing."

She had talked him into a corner with her logic. He shouldn't be surprised. She was the cleverest person he knew, aside perhaps from Brother Gilbert. But she was also damned frustrating. Why couldn't she just accept his explanation?

Ronan thrust another timber up against the ones that had been brought up already. The pyre shook with the force of the action, but 'twasn't enough to curb his frustration.

The only excuse he had left to him was the truest one. 'Twas also the one he knew would prick her temper the most, unfortunately. But she'd left him no choice. He could see her gearing up for her next barrage, so he told her what he knew she didn't want to hear.

"My father would never arrest a noble woman, or man, short of a murder charge. After it had happened, not before," he explained, "He'd never apprehend Lady Sybilla on our suspicions alone. Even with Lucy's testimony, the laird would never take action against her."

Ronan hadn't believed she could become any angrier. He was wrong. She looked fit to burst, like a forge that needed airing. The fire within her burned too hot, and he knew something had to give way. Quickly.

She grabbed the sticks she'd carried uphill, thrusting them one by one into the pyre with enough force to threaten the entire structure. She glared at the ground the entire time she worked.

"Adelina?" he was terrified to provoke her, but 'twas clear the conversation wasn't finished just yet.

"Of course," she whimpered. Her anger had dissipated in seconds, replaced now by the vulnerability hiding behind it.

Her sudden sadness hurt him more than her anger ever could.

She looked him dead in the eye. "Of course it's because she's a noble. How could you ever condemn your betrothed and threaten your future together? If 'twere me in her place, I'd be in chains the moment you spoke with Lucy."

Ronan's stomach lurched. That was not at all the reaction he'd expected. "Adelina, no," he fumbled for an explanation, a way to show her how wrong she was. But she knew he was grasping.

She raised her hands to stop him before he ever got started. When she looked at him again, the anger was back. She was burning. She was furious. She was fire incarnate. "If you won't tell the laird that his life is in danger, then, as his advisor, I will." She spoke with a strain, barely able to control her own voice in the face of her rage. Then she turned, and Ronan knew she'd walk straight to his father and get herself into trouble.

"I will tell him!" Ronan shouted before she could start back down the hill.

Adelina paused, turning to look at him.

"I will tell him," Ronan repeated, walking over to her, "but don't be surprised if he does nothing. He places great value on our alliance, and I doubt he'd cast that aside for hearsay."

"We'll find out, won't we," Adelina said. "I've had enough of fires. I'm going back to the library to see if I can finally make sense of that letter."

Ronan was relieved that she didn't plan to accompany him to speak with his father. 'Twas already going to be an unpleasant conversation, and he didn't need her short temper added to it.

"I'll find you once I have his answer," Ronan promised. Adelina went down the hill alone, far to the left of where they had climbed. She was no doubt heading to her cottage for the letter. Ronan hastened down to the keep to confront his father, hoping that the clan would see the night safely through.

Chapter Twenty-Five

Ronan entered the great hall ready for battle. He was certain his father wouldn't easily heed his warning about Lady Sybilla. Ronan himself hardly knew whether he believed her the traitor, but he had promised Adelina he would speak with his father. And they certainly didn't have any better leads. She'd been right that now was the time for action. Better that they try to stop the traitor than sit back and wait for chaos to descend.

Looking about the room, however, his father was nowhere in sight. 'Twas unusual for him to be elsewhere, as the great hall was the meeting place of the clan. If anyone needed to find the laird, the great hall was the place to look.

The fireplace roared behind the rows of trestle tables. A half-drunk goblet of ale waited patiently, the chair in front of it pulled away from the table's edge. His father had been in the room, and recently.

Growing concern urged Ronan further into the hall, toward the solar. What if the traitor had already gotten to the laird? Had it been Lady Sybilla? Could she really best his father, a great warrior?

By the time Ronan opened the door into the solar, he was overcome with worry. Nothing surprised him more than finding his father sitting across from Lady Sybilla and Lucy, engaged in civil conversation.

"You look like you've seen a ghost, lad," his father commented. "Come, join us. We were just discussing the wedding."

Ronan stepped into the room. "Father, you forget that we are not yet betrothed," he reminded as gently as he could manage. "And I had hoped to speak with you in private."

"I can't just dismiss these lovely ladies," his father argued, already frowning.

"No need, laird," Lady Sybilla said, rising from her chair, "I am happy to do my Ronan's bidding. A wife must be obedient, after all." She smiled at him sweetly as she and Lucy left the room.

Ronan closed the door and turned to face his father.

"This had better be good, boy," he warned, "I'm none too pleased at you tossing out your future wife."

He hadn't come here to mince words with his father, so he got right to it. "I believe 'tis possible that Lady Sybilla is the traitor named in the letter," he said.

The laird laughed gruffly. "Don't be ridiculous. What would make you think such a thing?"

"She has been seen during or directly after all of the attacks in the last week," Ronan explained.

"Attacks?" his father scoffed at the word. "You mean the riding accident? The intrusion at the library?"

"Well what else would you call them?" Ronan countered. "Adelina's cottage was broken into as well, if you'll remember."

His father's eyes narrowed. "Who saw her?" he questioned.

Ronan knew what the laird was up to. "Adelina saw her the morning she woke to find her cottage torn apart. We both saw her when the library was broken into, and I alone was there when we were riding."

"Adelina's word cannot be trusted," his father declared, "I believe 'tis just as likely that she is the traitor. She should have figured out that letter by now, if she's as clever as Brother Gilbert insists. For all I know she's withholding the information to protect herself."

"And what of my own word?" Ronan asked, refusing to be drawn into a petty argument over Adelina.

"Normally I would trust your word," his father began, "but I know how much you detest the idea of marriage. And though I'm certain you were thrown from your horse, there was no evidence of any trap on the path you were found."

"That's because Lady Sybilla took it down before she came for help," Ronan said. "Her maid, too, has expressed concern over Lady Sybilla's behavior of late."

"Oh, has she now? And what does the little maid have to say?"

Ronan could tell by his father's tone that he wasn't going to hear him out, but he pressed on anyway. "Lady Sybilla has been sneaking away from Lucy. Difficult to find, and evasive when asked about it. And Lady Sybilla has been asking suspicious questions about the Samhain fires and the posting of guards."

The laird looked at him for a long moment, then paced across the room several times, deep in thought.

"Even if what you say is true, I can do naught about it. The conjecture of two commoners and a disgruntled Highlander cannot condemn an English noblewoman."

'Twas a more reasonable answer than Ronan had expected, but no different in its sentiment. There was, however, one other matter he had planned to discuss with his father. He'd given it a great deal of thought, and realized that he couldn't marry Lady Sybilla. Every moment he'd spent with Lady Sybilla had convinced him that he couldn't tolerate her as a wife, regardless of his feelings on marriage. Now that he believed it was possible that she was plotting against his clan, he felt justified in telling his father as much.

"I'm not going to marry a traitor," Ronan proclaimed.

In a flash, his father's calm, reasonable demeanor gave way to beast-like rage. "Guards!" he roared, moving to trap Ronan in the room until they arrived.

"What are you doing?" Ronan asked, shocked at the ferocity of his father's reaction.

"You broke your word to me," his father growled. "I will do the same. Adelina is no longer my advisor, as she stayed here safely because of your vow to marry. As an oath breaker, you will join her in the holding cell until I decide on a fitting punishment."

His father's guards, Hugh and Bothan, entered the solar looking confused.

"Please escort Ronan to the holding cell. Then you may fetch Adelina to join him."

"Father, please," Ronan urged, "Let's discuss this further. I'm sure we can come to some agreement."

"Silence!" his father commanded, "There is nothing left for us to discuss."

Ronan, though furious with his father, saw no reason to give the lads a hard time. He walked beside them to the holding cell on the back of the keep. It had its own door and could not be accessed from the within the keep proper. A small, dark hallway led to a single cell with a reinforced oaken door. Both doors locked from the outside.

"Please be gentle with her," Ronan requested before Bothan locked him in. "Don't scare her."

"We'd rather not fetch her at all, Ronan, you know that," Bothan said somberly. "I feel badly enough about the other night."

"We'll bring her to you as best we can," Hugh assured him, "but that lass has some fire in her."

Ronan smiled sadly. "Yes," he agreed, "she certainly does."

Chapter Twenty-Six

Adelina fumed as she made her way from her cottage to the library. The village of Calder bustled all around her as everyone made ready for the evening's celebration. Fading leaves danced about her flowing skirts, tickling her legs and distracting her from her frustration with Ronan and the letter. Why couldn't he see reason? And why couldn't she figure out that last line?

The library was far enough away from the keep's courtyard that it afforded Adelina a measure of silence in which to work. The afternoon light was quickly disappearing, however, and she had to light a candle to read without straining her eyes. Some of the sheets Ronan had stacked yesterday belonged to Cicero's speeches. Though she'd been occupied since then, the pages had given her an idea.

Sitting down at the table with Ronan's plaid wrapped about her, Adelina laid out as many of the pages as she could find across the surface of the table. She had already tried everything she could think of. Twice now, she had gone back through her grammar books to be sure she wasn't completely missing some archaic word forms. She had rearranged the words, added and taken away letters, and still she could not determine what it said.

Armed with a new plan, Adelina picked up the page closest in the oration to the lines quoted in the letter. This time, instead of trying to find similar words, she looked for similar letter combinations. How Aidan could possibly have composed something so convoluted was beyond her. If she ever met him, she'd tell him as much.

She carefully read each phrase aloud, repeating it as she scanned the jumbled words of the letter. It almost looked as if he had started words without finishing them. Mayhap the endings were in the lines of Cicero.

Adelina went through several pages without much luck. Aye, she'd found a few matches here and there, but nothing that made any kind of sense. Until she read the end of a passage some ten pages past where she'd begun.

"*...dignum moribus factisque suis exitium vitae invenit*," she repeated aloud. And then she knew. "*Invenit*," she said again. The word rang in her ears. Looking at the last line of the letter, she realized exactly what Aidan had done. And it was nowhere near as complicated as anyone believed.

He had placed spaces between the wrong letters. The first word wasn't *inve*. It was *inveni*, the same verb Cicero had just used. Adelina wrote the entire line without any spaces, and in minutes she had her answer.

Inveni carduum et sicam. Proditor est. Find the thistle and dagger. That is the traitor.

Lucy! It was Lucy! She'd seen that very emblem on Lucy's cloak during their afternoon together.

Adelina's elation at solving the riddle dissolved into crushing defeat. If the traitor was Lucy, then it couldn't be Lady Sybilla. Which meant that Ronan could marry Lady Sybilla, who was right now being wrongly accused of multiple crimes. And, of course, it meant that Ronan was right. Lady Sybilla was innocent.

She had only hours to stop Lucy. Flying from her chair, Adelina grabbed the letter and readjusted her plaid, preparing to rush to the keep. Before she did anything else, she needed to find Ronan and tell him what she'd discovered. They could make amends with Lady Sybilla once they'd found Lucy.

Everything was going well for all of two minutes. Then she hurried out the door. And smack into Hugh and Bothan. Oh, aye, she knew them. After they'd as much as abducted her the night the letter arrived, they came by the following morning to apologize to her. Though they were well-intentioned, when they were out looking for her, Adelina knew there would be trouble. And she simply did not have time for trouble. So she ran.

She squeezed between them before they'd realized what had happened.

"Adelina! Please don't!" Hugh called.

"Come back!" Bothan pleaded.

She ignored them, putting as much distance between herself and the guards as she could. The effort of keeping Ronan's plaid draped about her was slowing her down. She dropped it, though her heart lurched the moment it left her.

Beleaguered groans sounded from behind her as Bothan and Hugh reluctantly gave chase. Their footfalls quickly caught up to her. A hand reached from behind, and nearly grabbed a fistful of her dress.

They were going to catch her. If Adelina continued the way she was going, she'd be captured in moments. Instead, she turned a quick corner. She sped up just enough to dart in front of Bothan without getting bowled over.

She sprinted down the short alleyway. Bales of hay and straw lined the hard-packed dirt. Stray pieces of straw crunched grotesquely underfoot as she ran. Adelina took the next possible turn, now running straight toward the courtyard.

'Twas a good distance to the keep. Several cottages, the stable, and the blacksmith laid end to end between Adelina and her destination. The road had not fared well with all the rain of late, and Adelina had to slow her gait to avoid wrenching an ankle. An assortment of barrels were strewn about, most in close proximity to the stable and blacksmith. The blacksmith also kept his woodpile on this side of the building.

A hooded figure with the gait of a woman crossed the courtyard perpendicular to Adelina, headed toward the keep. The woman approached the stone steps, glancing left and right before she walked around the side of the building, away from Adelina.

Adelina's eyes were pinned to the woman. She was blind to all else. It must be Lucy, readying her trap for the laird. There was no time to lose. Pushing herself with all she had left, Adelina ran faster than she'd ever run before. Everyone was depending upon her.

She never took her eyes off Lucy. Until her foot got stuck in a rut. Adelina tumbled forward, losing sight of Lucy as well as her lead in the chase. Before she could stand back up, Hugh and Bothan had her arms. They helped her to stand, but they looked none too pleased with her.

"What did I do this time?" Adelina demanded, trying to tug her arms free of their iron grasp.

"I don't think 'twas you, lass," Hugh said gruffly. "'Twas Ronan."

Adelina sagged in defeat. She'd gotten him into trouble over Lady Sybilla, and for nothing. "I must speak with him," she told them.

"Oh, you'll have plenty of time to speak with him," Bothan answered her cryptically as they led her toward the keep.

What could she possibly say to Ronan? Adelina's mind raced, searching for the words to explain everything to Ronan. She needed to set things right between them. By the time they reached a dreary little door on the back of the keep, Adelina knew she was in for a long day.

Chapter Twenty-Seven

Cold stone walls surrounded her, a hard earthen floor beneath her feet. The holding cell was but one small chamber and its connecting entry hall. Both locked from the outside. Ronan stood brooding in the far right corner, arms crossed as usual. The wooden door closed behind her, the lock clicking into place with ringing finality.

Adelina turned round and banged twice on the door. "I'm getting awfully tired of being manhandled by the two of you!" she shouted angrily.

"Then don't run next time!" came a muffled reply from the other side. She couldn't even tell which of them had said it.

"You ran?" Ronan asked with exasperation.

"Of course I ran," Adelina replied. "What did you expect me to do? Walk quietly to my cell?"

Ronan let out a snort of ironic laughter. "No," he answered, "Certainly not."

"Ronan, we have to get out of here," Adelina said, suddenly remembering what she had been on her way to tell him in the first place.

"Not to be demeaning," Ronan said, "but isn't that a tad obvious?"

"Ugh!" Adelina cried. "I mean, we have to stop Lucy! We only have a few hours before they'll be starting the fires."

"Lucy?" Ronan asked, changing position for the first time since she'd entered the cell.

"Aye," Adelina agreed reluctantly. "I owe you an apology. You were right. Lady Sybilla was innocent."

"You're certain?" he pressed.

"I finally read the last line," Adelina explained. "It's definitely Lucy."

Ronan exhaled deeply. He wandered over to the only window, high in the cell near the ceiling. "I can't see a thing," he grumbled. Even on his toes his eyes were not quite level with the bottom of it.

"If you lifted me up, I could see if anyone's there," Adelina suggested.

Moments later, Ronan had lifted her by the waist up to his right shoulder. His right arm kept her from tumbling off, and his left hand held her legs firmly to his chest.

Two steel rods blocked any attempts at escape out the window, but they served as useful grips for Adelina to help hold her weight. Ignoring the incredible discomfort of her precarious perch, she scanned the narrow view for anyone who could help.

The window didn't give much of a view of anything, save the side of the brewery. Adelina couldn't quite see around a corner to where she knew the courtyard lay. It appeared most of the villagers had begun heading toward the hillside to await sunset.

"Is anyone there?" Ronan asked when she hadn't said a word in several minutes.

"Not a soul," Adelina replied sadly.

He gently lowered her to the ground again, and quickly removed his hands from her. Too quickly.

"What do we do?" Adelina asked, trying not to dwell on the fact that even now he didn't dare touch her.

"We wait," Ronan mumbled.

"We could talk," Adelina offered, sitting as comfortably as she could on the damp, dusty floor.

Ronan gave her a skeptical look. "About what?"

"Are you going to marry Lady Sybilla now?" Adelina asked. "Now that you know she's not the traitor?" Though she was terrified of his answer, she knew she needed to hear it.

"I don't know," he answered.

Her heart ached at the uncertainty of his answer. It meant he was at least considering it. Perhaps it was the closeness of the cell or the desperate situation in which she found herself. Either way, Adelina finally found the courage to ask the question that had been following her, taunting her. "Are you going to marry me?"

Ronan looked at the ground. "No, lass," he whispered. "I can't."

Adelina's chest tightened. She could hardly take a breath. "No," she said, her voice cracking, "I suppose you couldn't. Then you'd risk losing your beloved Lady Sybilla."

"Beloved?" Ronan cried, running his hands through his disheveled brown hair, "Adelina, do not for one moment confuse station with affection."

"And why not?" she retorted, rising to her feet. "You bed me once and cast me aside, then all you can do is speak on behalf of *Lady* Sybilla. You yourself admitted it was because she's noble born. 'Tis obvious you care for her."

Ronan's muscles tensed. "You believe I care for Lady Sybilla in place of you?" he asked.

"As I said," Adelina answered sullenly, "'tis obvious."

Ronan sighed, a deep heavy sound full of some emotion Adelina couldn't quite name. "I don't know if I'll marry Lady Sybilla," he repeated, "and my feelings have nothing to do with it. As to my feelings for you, there is nothing between us save mistakes."

Adelina shrunk back into the corner, defeated. What a fool she had been, to think he would choose her over a noblewoman. To believe in the smallest possibility that he might marry her. To believe he loved her.

He had spent hardly a moment with Adelina after she shared his bed. As much as it broke her heart, Adelina was beginning to see the reality of her situation. Brother Gilbert had warned her, and he'd been right. Ronan could never love someone of common birth.

Was she stupid, to have believed him in love with her? Mayhap that was naïveté. She hadn't expected him to marry her. Hoped mayhap, but not expected. Adelina pulled her arms more tightly about herself, pathetically attempting to fight off the bitter cold. It was still an hour before sunset. By nightfall, it would be far worse.

At least one hour passed in wretched silence. Ronan brooded over Lord knows what, stalking around the cell relentlessly. He never even looked at her again. All the time in the world, and he didn't bother with any more of an explanation. He had apparently said all that was necessary.

Outside, Adelina could tell almost exactly the moment of the sunset. Cheers rang out from far beyond Calder Keep, sweeping down the surrounding hillsides and echoing over the courtyard to the walls of the small holding cell. The entire world was oblivious to the misery hanging in the air between them.

A shout went up.

Adelina's ears twitched. It didn't sound quite right.

Screams soon followed, first from a great distance and then right across the courtyard.

She slid up the wall, rising to her feet. There was a single window, high in the cell near the ceiling. Ronan was in front of it in two long strides. Gripping the bars of the window, he pulled himself up by his arms so that he could finally see though the tiny opening.

Adelina's curiosity burned, but not badly enough to speak with Ronan. She backed up as far away from the window as she could manage, hoping a different angle might afford her a view of something other than the purple hues of dusk. Craning her neck and up on her toes, squished into the far corner of the cell, Adelina caught the telltale flicker of firelight.

A wisp of smoke rose, followed by a great billow. The screaming picked up its cadence, always reaching a crescendo just as another billow strayed into sight. The fire couldn't be from any of the pyres, for it was much too close and in the wrong direction. A sick feeling settled in Adelina's belly as the realization struck her. The keep was on fire.

Ronan turned to her for the first time since their argument. "We need to get out of here," he growled. He turned and rushed at the door, barreling into it with his shoulder. It shook and creaked, but didn't break. He groaned in pain, walking back to the wall. Then he ran at it again. A screech of surprise sounded from the other side of the doorway. The lock clicked open.

Ronan walked to stand between Adelina and the opening door. His stance told her he was ready to tear apart whatever came through that door.

"There you are!" Lady Sybilla shouted. She sighed, taking a moment to catch her breath. Then she rushed over to Ronan and grabbed his arm, tugging him toward the open door.

"We have to hurry! There's no time to spare!" she urged.

"What are you doing here?" Adelina snapped from behind Ronan.

"Well, that's no way to greet your rescuer," Lady Sybilla said with entirely too much decorum. No one had the right to be so composed while the world turned to fire all around.

"Where's the laird?" Adelina demanded.

"Honestly," Lady Sybilla said, her feet dancing anxiously, "we haven't the time to sort that out just now. The fire is spreading quickly. I heard your father had locked you in here, and I had to be sure you got out. You're lucky, too. Your guards were nowhere to be found."

"Which we appreciate," Ronan said, glaring daggers at Adelina. "Where is Lucy?" he asked, looking back to Lady Sybilla.

"I can't find her anywhere," Lady Sybilla admitted. Her voice rang of defeat. "I looked, really I did. I hope she managed to get away in time."

"Where did you last see her?" Adelina questioned.

Lady Sybilla thought for a moment. "I haven't seen her since this morning," she replied. "I assumed that perhaps she'd met someone she fancied."

"We have to find Lucy before she kills my father," Ronan said, pushing past Lady Sybilla as he shot out of the cell.

"What!" Lady Sybilla shouted, her plea for decorum apparently forgotten.

"We haven't the time, Sybilla," Adelina answered tartly. She grabbed Lady Sybilla's hand and pulled her out the door after Ronan.

Chapter Twenty-Eight

Ronan stopped just outside the cell, staring blankly into the chaos before them. Everything was on fire. Flames lit up the night from the courtyard to the hillside beyond. Horses bolted from the stables, dancing across hot stone. The force of the heat was so great that it created its own burning wind. The three of them stood together, watching the Highlands burn.

"We should get to the central pyre," Lady Sybilla shouted over the commotion. "Laird Murdoch was on his way there to say the blessings when this all started."

Ronan nodded his head, and they took off. Halfway across the courtyard, Ronan realized that Adelina had not followed.

"What are you doing?" he bellowed.

"You two go on," she said, "I'll look somewhere else."

"Absolutely not," Ronan growled, reaching to yank her along with him.

"'Tis not safe to be on your own," Lady Sybilla agreed.

Adelina's stomach turned. She couldn't stand to be around Ronan, let alone while he played nice with Lady Sybilla. She needed to get as far from the pair of them as she could, and quickly. "I'm not beholden to either one of you," Adelina stated. She looked Ronan dead in the eyes. "And the last thing I'd want is for you to make yet another mistake."

Ronan dropped her arm. He backed away like he'd been struck, then turned to head up the hill in search of his father. Lady Sybilla looked concerned about leaving Adelina, but she followed Ronan moments later.

As much as she desired to wallow in self-pity and anger, Adelina had more important problems at hand. If she had paid more attention to ferreting out the traitor and less attention to her traitorous heart, mayhap she could have avoided this night altogether. Now all she could do was act quickly before the fire made searching impossible.

Taking stock of the dire situation which surrounded her, Adelina determined that the keep would be the best place to search for the laird. Well, not the safest, certainly, but the most likely place to find him. If she had to wager on it, Adelina would guess that Lucy set fire in the courtyard to get the laird's attention on his way up the hill. Then she lured him into the keep and set fire to that with him inside. At least, that seemed to Adelina the only way someone so small and unassuming could best a beastly warrior like Laird Calder.

Having made up her mind, Adelina charged toward the keep. Red-orange flames swirled a wicked dance of destruction. Every way she looked, Adelina's vision was tinged by straying flares. Acrid smoke filled her nose. She choked on each breath as she ran to the heart of the fire. As she neared the main entry into the great hall, a sinking feeling came over Adelina.

Where once the great oaken doors stood guardian to the entrance, there now burned a ring of fire, leading into a chasm of leaping flames. Adelina couldn't even tell if the floor was still intact, let alone how she might navigate her way inside. Turning away to look elsewhere, the unmistakable roar of the laird swearing an oath caught her attention. He was inside.

The cacophony surrounding her nearly overwhelmed the laird's voice, a phenomenon she hadn't believed possible. The noise was such that she could tell he was inside the keep, but she couldn't pinpoint what room, or even which floor, he was within. One way or another, Adelina had to get inside the keep. The last time she couldn't get in through the great hall, she had snuck in through the kitchens. Without a second thought, Adelina took off in the direction of the garden.

She tore through the beds, nearly tripping over a few corners in the darkness. If not for the conflagration behind her lighting the night, she'd have fallen flat on her face onto the stone walkway.

The door into the kitchen was open, likely due to a hasty exit by the servants. Inside, the room was dark and cold. Chopped leeks sat waiting next to a stew pot. A pile of honey cakes had half-tumbled from its serving tray. Adelina spotted a waterskin that someone had dropped and slung it over her shoulder. There wasn't a lot of water, but it could be useful in a pinch.

Quickly taking stock of her surroundings, Adelina noted that the door between the great hall and the kitchen was closed. She approached it cautiously, reaching to open it. When her hand touched the handle, 'twas burning hot. She backed away quickly, her hand as hot as if she'd grabbed a candle flame. If she opened that door, she'd get a face full of fire. She couldn't get in through the kitchen.

She could, however, tell that the laird was somewhere on the first floor on the opposite side of the hall, likely in the solar or his quarters. Time was moving swiftly, and Adelina wasn't. She ran back outside, heart racing. What if she didn't get to him in time? What if the building collapsed upon both of them and she met a fiery end this very night? What if she had to tell Ronan she'd watched his father perish, unable to save him?

She couldn't. Those were simply not options. She would press on, and she would find the laird, and they would both escape. Adelina made the sign of the cross and sent a hasty prayer heavenward, for what it was worth on such short notice. Running across the courtyard to the side of the keep where the family's rooms lay, she stared at the gray stone walls between herself and Laird Murdoch.

Normally, the stone walls are washed in a slick coating of lime, and the mortar is fitted tightly enough to make scaling them difficult. But the mortar was cracking, the stones shifting. The fire had burned so hot, it was threatening to collapse even the stone walls. Adelina was no mason, but even she could tell the wall would be in pieces before sunrise. Already it bowed outward precariously.

Another shout from the laird, much closer than before, pushed Adelina to action. She fitted her hands into two crevices just above her head and lifted herself up until she found a set of footholds. Then she kept climbing, never looking back.

A window one floor up the tower, appeared free of fire. She had no idea how she would get from that room to the laird, but she'd have to sort that out once she could think clearly. Currently, she was trying not to fall to her death. Alright, mayhap the fall wouldn't kill her, but it would hurt.

Adelina's shoulders ached. She pushed herself up with her legs as much as she could, but 'twas impossible to move without also using her arms. Apparently she didn't use them that often, for they felt weak and shaky after only minutes of her climb. Faster would be better, she decided. She'd be tired and sore either way, so she may as well get on with it. The stones shifted beneath her fingers more and more as she neared the window above.

Just as she neared the level of the window, her foot slipped. Adelina screamed in shock, but caught herself on the window's ledge. Hanging in midair, her feet worked the stone in front of her over and over, moving like a wheel until she found some purchase. A push, a jump, and a pull and she was tumbling headfirst into the room. The laird had better write her letter now, she thought. If this didn't earn his respect, surely nothing could.

Forcing herself to stand, Adelina looked around the room. Lady Sybilla's room. Of course. As she'd hoped, the fire hadn't reached this section of the keep yet. The laird was yelling again, this time his voice had an urgency to it that Adelina hadn't noted before. After a quick scan of the room, she went to open the door. This time, there was no heat on the other side and she opened it.

The far side of the hallway and the staircase burned, and the inferno crept ominously toward her. Minutes. She had minutes to sort this out. The laird was one floor below her, almost exactly. The only way out of the solar was through the great hall, which was impossible now. A plan formed, and Adelina took action.

First, she ran back to Lady Sybilla's room. She tied together the sheets from the two beds, then tied them to the bed frame nearest the door. Next, she rolled a large log from the fireplace into the hallway. Then she grabbed a fireplace hook and ran back into the hall.

She wedged the hook beneath a warping floorboard in the hallway, placing the log beneath it to create a lever. She'd seen something similar in one of the illustrations in Vitruvius' tome on Roman architecture. With a deep, trembling breath, she knelt on the floor, using all her weight to push down on the back end of the hook. The board creaked and lifted, but not enough.

"Again!" she heard the laird shout below her. "Do it again!"

She could do this. Lord, how her body ached. Everything hurt and sweat poured from every inch of her body. The keep was hotter than midsummer in the south of England. But she knew the laird's life depended on her. So she pushed again, and again, and again. With as much haste as she could, she lifted the hallway floor until she could make out the laird waiting below her. He had piled two chairs, and was reaching to poke holes of his own, now that he knew he had aid.

"You?!" he screamed in surprise.

Adelina knew he meant no ill will by it. Yet she couldn't suppress her annoyance that he was still plagued by such pettiness when his life was under threat. "Don't you start with me, laird," she growled right back at him. She slammed the hook handle to the floor a final time to punctuate her frustration. A hole wide enough for the laird opened, and she ran to retrieve the bed sheet rope she'd fashioned.

She threw it down to him, only then realizing that he was catching fire at an alarming rate. He screamed in agony as he climbed, and she had to help pull him up. Using the sheets as best she could, Adelina pushed the laird to the ground and put out the fire from his clothes. She had just enough time to drag him to the window with the sheets before the fire reached the hall outside the room.

"You must climb!" she shouted at him.

His eyes were glassy, unfocused from the pain of his burns. She slapped him across the cheek, hard enough to leave a mark. Anger flickered in his eyes, and she knew he was registering her instructions now.

"Grab the sheets. Hold on tight. Get your arse to the bottom, and then you can wallow in pain," she ordered.

"You've a mouth on ye, lass," he slurred out, his words running together in the heaviest brogue she'd heard yet.

They hadn't much time. She tied the sheets around his waist, though she doubted that alone could hold him if he slipped. Mayhap 'twould slow his fall, at least. Then she spun him around and helped him drop out the window.

He had enough presence of mind to grab on to the sheet and try to find footholds. Adelina scaled down the wall, reaching for the sheet whenever she slipped. Each time she yanked on it, she felt it give a little more. The laird was several feet above the ground, but the fall wouldn't kill him. He was safe for now.

Adelina looked back up just in time to see the first blocks of stone tumble from the wall above her, landing with a thud on the ground below. Her time was up. She let go of the wall, sliding with no grace whatsoever down the last feet of the bed sheets. Adelina glanced up in time to see the entire castle wall hurling toward them.

Chapter Twenty-Nine

Ronan stalked the hilltops surrounding the village, looking everywhere for his father and Lucy. They hadn't been on the central hill, where the largest pyre stood aflame. He'd checked the next nearest one, still without luck. His search was growing frenzied as the minutes passed without any progress. How could he rescue his father if he couldn't find him? How could he stop Lucy?

"Ronan?" Lady Sybilla's voice broke his concentration.

"What?" he growled. He didn't have time to chat. He needed to find them before it was too late.

"Ronan!" Lady Sybilla shouted.

He turned grumpily to look at her. Whatever she wanted, it had better be worth the interruption.

She pointed toward the keep. It took Ronan several moments to see what she was trying to show him. And then he felt the blood drain from his face.

Ronan watched in horror. Helpless. He watched Adelina, that crazy, incredible lass, *scale a castle wall.* When he realized what she was up to, he ran so fast he nearly tumbled down the hillside. She needed help. He needed to be there.

Lady Sybilla followed close on his heels. For a gentlewoman, she was astonishingly quick.

"We need to go the other way!" she called. "Around the fire!"

Deciding that urgency was a top priority, he nodded, changing course to follow her and circumvent the conflagration sooner rather than later. He glanced up briefly to check on Adelina. Before he had time to revert his gaze, Lady Sybilla screamed. She had turned a corner up near the keep and he'd lost sight of her.

"Ronan, help!" Lady Sybilla cried. He could hear her struggling. She wasn't alone.

He caught sight of Lucy, dragging Lady Sybilla toward the stables 'round the back way. She hadn't seen him.

Ronan swore under his breath. He'd had just about enough of this day. He was finished with it when Adelina had argued with him on the hilltop. Everything after that was simply ridiculous. With a groan of frustration, Ronan launched himself off the rubble, racing back through the courtyard to head them off.

When he turned the corner into what remained of the stables, he was greeted by a surprised Lucy. Lady Sybilla struggled against her captor viciously. Ronan started toward them, intending to make quick work of it, when Lucy unsheathed a dagger and held it to Lady Sybilla's throat.

All about them, fires blazed. Most of the horses had fled long ago, but a few poor beasts remained locked in their stalls. A portion of the building had long since collapsed. The fire had already reached its peak here, and was smoldering happily as any bonfire might. Every so often another section of wall collapsed, but Ronan's attention was on the women before him.

"Lucy," he said through gritted teeth, "Spare the lady's life, and you'll have a fair trial, by my word." He hoped that if he remained calm, she would also. The last thing he needed was a murdered Englishwoman on Calder lands.

Lucy scoffed at Ronan. "Trial!" she shouted, "For what?"

Lady Sybilla inhaled sharply as the blade moved.

Ronan rolled his lips to keep from shouting at her. Mayhap she was addled. "Treachery," he reminded her fiercely, "attempted murder, arson. The list grows with each passing moment, lass."

"The only traitor in Calder Keep is that bastard of a laird!" she screeched, "Death is a fitting punishment for courting the English while our king meets them on the battlefield!"

Lord, she was addled. "Lucy," Ronan argued, "you know as well as I that the war with England 'tis naught but a family squabble. Clan Calder has always stood behind Kind David in battle."

She spat at him, a viper unleashing her venom. "'Tis not the usurper David of whom I speak," she seethed, "Malcolm is the true King of Scotland."

"Malcolm lost his inheritance in battle," Ronan retorted, "Were he stronger, he would, indeed, be our king." In truth, Ronan couldn't care a whit over which of the bastards claimed the title. So far Clan Calder was out of reach of either. As long as things stayed that way, he'd support whoever won the battles.

"I take it you've lost no brothers in battle, then," Lucy countered, "You've not seen the women weeping over men who'll never return. You'd not speak so casually of war with England if you'd seen it yourself."

"War is never kind," Ronan argued, "but you can be. You can rise above it. Let the lady go."

Lucy was silent. Her dagger still. For the briefest moment, Ronan thought he had her. And then her eyes flickered, moving first one way and then another. She was calculating. Ronan had seen many a warrior do the same. She was going to run.

Everything happened at once, a jumble of stalled actions tumbling out too quickly. Ronan rushed to intercept Lucy. She'd likely make for one of the remaining horses, and she'd need to mount it before she could flee. Lady Sybilla spun about as Lucy's grip shifted. She shoved Lucy, desperate to create space between them. Lucy started to run toward a horse, but not before she stabbed Lady Sybilla in the side. Lady Sybilla crumpled to the ground, blood gushing from her side.

Ronan jumped toward Lucy to stop her escape. As he did, he caught a glimpse of the same wall Adelina had been scaling. He stopped in his tracks, watching her toss his father out the window in a bed sheet. *A bed sheet.*

He stared in disbelief at the ridiculous rescue underway. The woman was a either brilliant or daft. In the midst of his shock, as they dangled only feet above the ground, the entire wall collapsed on top of them.

Ronan's heart nearly stopped. His breath came heavy, paining him with each motion. He fought the urge to run straight to the collapsed keep. Straight to Adelina. Straight to his father. The sound of hoof beats brought him back to the present, alerting him to Lucy's successful escape. He tore his gaze from the crumbling keep in time to see her galloping out of the stable.

Lady Sybilla needed immediate attention or she would bleed to death. Gasping in pain, her face grew paler each second. Ronan tore off his shirt, tying it tightly about her waist to staunch the flow of blood. He knew he ought not move someone in her condition, but he could hardly leave her inside a burning building next to a collapsing keep. She shrieked in pain as he lifted her, then blessedly passed out. Fintan, whom he'd hardly seen over the last days, found him before he'd carried her ten paces.

"I'll take her," Fintan offered, shifting her into his arms and carrying her away from the stables. "I'll be back when she's settled."

Ronan flew to the wreckage, throwing aside stones and fighting his rising panic. They couldn't be dead. He couldn't lose them.

The stones rose high before him. Aye they tumbled to the ground, but piled atop one another they were half as high as the full tower had been. A mountain of rubble lay before him. He needed to keep moving stones, needed to keep digging deeper. Yet he also needed to venture toward the center of the stones to see if they had somehow ended up further from where he'd last seen them.

Folk had begun cautiously returning to the courtyard and the surrounding village, taking stock of what was lost to them and looking for injured relatives. As Ronan tossed stone after stone, he noted that a bucket chain had begun to retrieve water from the nearest loch, over a quarter mile into the hills. Though commendable, their efforts were hardly enough to put out such a great conflagration.

Hours passed. Ronan's hands had broken open, and blood now covered each stone he moved. Several warriors had come to join him in his search. None said a word, until just before dawn.

"Ronan!" Fintan shouted. He had been climbing about the far side of the rubble, helping to search after he'd returned from finding aid for Lady Sybilla.

Ronan sprinted up the pile of stone to where Fintan kneeled at an alcove. Ronan's father lay on the ground, protected by the outcropping from falling debris. The laird was unconscious and badly burned, but clearly breathing. He didn't have any obvious wounds from the stones, a good sign. Several women, who had been bringing buckets of water to the village, rushed over to help tend their laird.

Satisfied that he was in good hands and there was no more Ronan could do, he returned to the pile of stones. Knowing that his father had been on this side, Ronan realized he had likely been searching in the wrong spot for the better part of the night. With renewed vigor, he tore through the stones next to Fintan.

"Adelina!" he called frantically. He could feel desperation overtaking his actions. He was moving more wildly, taking less care. He was somehow slowing down and speeding up all at once. His hands were covered in blood, worked raw in his efforts to find her. "Adelina!" he tried again. And again. No matter how many times he cried her name, no reply ever came.

Ronan moved stones until he thought of nothing but endless mountains of gray. When finally the dawn rose, he fell to his knees, defeated. He had lost her.

Chapter Thirty

Samhain – October 31, 1136

Ronan's world lay in ruins about his feet. Most of the village surrounding Calder Keep was rubble and ash. His father was gravely wounded, hardly able to move half his body. Lady Sybilla barely clung to life. Only time would tell whether she would survive the coming days. She had lost too much blood, even after Ronan's efforts to staunch the flow. It had taken the efforts and knowledge of several villagers to keep her wound from gushing, and by then she'd grown pale and cold. Even if she recovered, Ronan wagered she'd never be as strong again. And Adelina. He couldn't even allow himself to think on her.

Once it was clear that Laird Murdoch wasn't in any condition to lead the clan during this turmoil, the clan had turned to Ronan for direction. He had called all who could be spared from the outlying villages to gather at the keep. They would be rebuilding all the cottages that were burned in the fire. Freezing weather and winter frosts would arrive in weeks, and half the clan would die of exposure if they had no homes to protect them.

By midafternoon on Samhain over a hundred clansmen had come from the outskirts of Calder lands to offer aid. Fingal and his mother Brigit were among the first to arrive. Ronan had Fingal gathering as much straw as could be found and delivering it to cottages that were only in need of new thatching on the roof. The furthest homes from the keep had fared the best, with only the roofs and windows catching fire, and many of those put out quickly. Closer to the keep, another group of villagers worked to clear debris and rebuild the first of many cottages from the ground up.

"Laird?"

Ronan turned to Fingal, the young lad whose family he'd visited with Adelina what seemed a lifetime ago. Fingal stood waiting for instructions with his arms full of straw. "Take it to Donal's cottage. 'Tis large enough for guests should we not be done before the weather turns."

Ronan himself helped to clear debris around the houses closest to the keep, those who had lost everything. He was among the strongest clansmen, so he took upon himself the most strenuous tasks. The laird's warriors, some of whom had thrown Ronan and Adelina in a holding cell not a day ago, now worked alongside him under his command. He carried stones, charred logs, and broken belongings. What they once had been, 'twas sometimes difficult to tell.

All the while, he couldn't let himself think of Adelina. He walked the rubble, trying to keep his guilt at bay. He knew he was responsible for her death. Not directly, mayhap, but it did not matter how he had contributed. It mattered only that she was gone.

He could not afford to weigh himself down with such thoughts. Nay, he scowled, picking up yet another charred cradle. 'Twas the fourth since sunrise, and every time he found one, he hunted down that family to ensure the child had survived the fire. Thus far, everyone was accounted for. Except Adelina, he thought miserably.

If only he had been with her, rescuing his father. If only he had run faster, gotten to her sooner. If only he had listened to her, had convinced her that he cared for her and not Lady Sybilla. If only he had told her that he loved her. If only he had asked her to marry him, none of this would have happened. He had tried so damned hard to push her away to save her from his own fears. Instead he pushed her straight to her own death.

"It looks as though your Samhain was taken over by the devil himself," a grim voice commented from behind him.

Ronan turned to see a familiar black-robed Benedictine. Normally he would've been overjoyed at Brother Gilbert's unexpected return. This day, he could hardly muster a smile.

"Something like that," Ronan muttered, turning quickly back to his work.

"What can we do to help you, cousin?" A tall, dark-haired warrior dismounted from a brown destrier.

Ronan stopped, regarding the man. Good Lord, 'twas Aidan. The last time Ronan had seen the lad he was playing at battle with the other children. The last time anyone at all had seen Aidan was nigh on two years past. Now he was a man full-grown. Ronan strode over to greet him, grasping his forearm, still in shock.

"You've grown," he said.

"'Twas nearly six years ago when last we met," Aidan answered with a smile, "'Twould be a concern if I hadn't."

Ronan looked around now, realizing that several MacMaster warriors had come with his cousin. "What are you doing here?" he asked incredulously. "Where have you been?"

Aidan grew serious. "'Tis a long tale," he replied. "Let us simply say that I'm here to help. We can save the details for a happier time."

Ronan nodded. He had many questions for his newly recovered

cousin, but 'twould seem the answers must wait. "Your aid is appreciated," he said. Ronan turned to Brother Gilbert, then. "And how is it you've come back to us once more?" he queried.

Brother Gilbert motioned to Aidan. "I was in the right place at the right time, as they say. I saw flames much too great rising from within Calder lands and headed toward them. I happened upon Aidan and his men along the way."

Ronan set the MacMaster men to work clearing rubble where cottages had once been, so that the villagers could start building. Almost as soon as he'd finished speaking the group of warriors had begun their task. He nodded his thanks to Aidan, then bent to pick up a large timber from the rubble nearby.

Brother Gilbert cleared his throat. Loudly.

"Yes?" Ronan acknowledged him in word, but continued carrying the timber to a pile out of the way.

"How is your father?" Brother Gilbert's question was tentative, his voice quiet. "I heard he was injured in the fire."

"He'll live," Ronan answered, "But only just."

Brother Gilbert frowned. "I'm sorry," he said. "I hadn't heard 'twas so serious. I assume you're laird in his stead?"

"Aye," Ronan replied.

Yet still Brother Gilbert lingered. He picked up smaller debris, moving it to the pile Ronan was building near the courtyard. He said nothing, simply worked alongside Ronan until 'twas getting on toward supper.

Normally, Ronan would have been overjoyed at the return of his dear friend. But on this one day, Ronan would have preferred solitude. When he was alone, 'twas easy to focus on his efforts and not allow his mind to wander into uncomfortable places. But with Brother Gilbert shadowing him, throwing meaningful glances his direction every so often, Ronan spent much of the afternoon wondering what it was Brother Gilbert wanted. For he knew the man was up to something.

Likely he wondered about Adelina. The two of them had grown fond of one another while he helped her settle in. And Ronan recalled well how Brother Gilbert had freely offered his commentary on their relationship. Then Ronan realized that he wasn't the only one who'd be missing her. Brother Gilbert deserved to know what had happened.

"We'll be needing you to say the rites," Ronan choked out, "for Adelina."

"For a marriage?" Brother Gilbert asked in shock.

Ronan would sooner die than continue this conversation, but he owed so much to Adelina. 'Twas the last thing he could do for her, so he pressed on. "For a funeral," he corrected, his throat going dry, "once we find her." He couldn't bring himself to look at Brother Gilbert. The man would surely be devastated as well.

"She died?" he asked skeptically.

"Aye," Ronan replied sullenly, "the keep fell upon her and my father. She saved his life, but I was not there to save hers."

"Did you quarrel before the fire?" he pressed.

If he hadn't been a man of God, Ronan would've knocked him unconscious by now. He knew from past conversations, however, that Brother Gilbert wouldn't leave it be.

"Aye, we quarreled," he ground out. "I told her I'd not marry her. 'Twas a fool's argument."

Brother Gilbert shook his head. "Not a fool," he corrected, "a coward."

Ronan bristled at that, stalking toward Brother Gilbert, who didn't give an inch.

"Be as angry as you want," he said calmly, "but try to tell me I'm wrong."

"You're wrong," Ronan replied without missing a beat. He could feel his pulse quickening, as though readying him for battle.

"So 'twasn't your fear of losing her in childbirth that kept you from taking vows?" Brother Gilbert countered.

Lord, was he ever frustrating. Always Brother Gilbert offered unwanted advice. And always 'twas the truth.

"I knew I shouldn't have spoken of it with you," Ronan said petulantly.

Brother Gilbert began to pace, his hands clasped behind his back, as he always did when he was teaching. "To submit to love is to risk great loss," he intoned, "If you had another chance with her, what would you do?"

"Does it matter?" Ronan sighed.

"You tell me," Brother Gilbert said, still pacing.

A groan of frustration escaped from Ronan, but he caved. "I'd marry her before she thought better of it," he said sadly. Lord what mistake he'd made.

"Well," Brother Gilbert said, "'tis your lucky day, lad."

Chapter Thirty-One

The wall gave way too quickly. Adelina had hoped they'd have longer to get to the ground and further from the building. Instead, she had to improvise.

She knew it was a risk, but it was all she had. Letting go of the wall, Adelina slid down the sheet. Her first instinct was to untie the knot, but she couldn't loosen it while he was suspended mid-air. It was too tight.

Looking up, she saw the stones beginning to fall. Glancing around, she saw the laird swinging just beneath her. They were nearly parallel to the window Ronan had spoken of in the library. Before the fire, it had been a beautiful masterpiece of stained glass artistry. The heat had shattered it, leaving an empty archway in its place. A keystone archway.

Adelina shoved the laird with everything she had left, propelling them both beneath the keystone. She held him in both arms to keep him steady. A raging inferno burned inside the great hall behind them. The heat alone was beginning to singe Adelina's dress, but she didn't have to endure it long. Just as they landed in the window's frame, the wall collapsed in a storm of rock and grit. The stones crumbled, boulders the size of her torso falling about them on all sides. The archway shook above them, but the keystone held. They were safe.

With great effort, certainly the last of her waning strength, she'd dragged the laird to an outcropping of stone nearby. It was far enough away that he'd not be injured if any more stones fell, at least.

A commotion rose up on the other side of the gigantic pile of rubble. A multitude of voices spoke and shouted, and Adelina instantly recognized one of them. Ronan was calling her name.

For just a moment, her heart swelled. He was worried about her. He was looking for her. Then she remembered their conversation. Of course he was worried. Any decent person would want to be certain she was safe. Nothing had changed. He didn't want to marry her. She was just a mistake.

Adelina Matheson was many things, but she refused to live her life as someone's 'mistake'. She hadn't the faintest idea what she would do next, but she knew with thunderous finality that her time as the scholar of Calder Keep had ended. So she ran.

Sooner than she'd expected, she was out in the wilds of the Highlands, far from the blazing village. Far from Ronan and Lady Sybilla, but not far enough. Not yet.

She kept going, happening upon one of the loose horses and deciding that she had no qualms over borrowing it. She'd see the gentle mare returned as soon as she was able. For now, she needed the horse's legs or she'd not make it far.

Adelina spent a good half hour figuring out how to mount a horse without a saddle or block. She'd ridden without a saddle once before, but it had been years ago when she was but a child. If she'd had more energy, she may have been more concerned over the ordeal. Instead, she grabbed a handful of mane and prayed to the good Lord she'd stay upright. She needed to use her thighs a good deal more than when the horse was saddled, but she found the mare more responsive than she would have expected.

Most of the ride was a blur of panic, pain, and darkness. By the time dawn broke the monotony of her journey, she stumbled into Brother Gilbert and a band of warriors, headed into Calder to offer aid.

"Lass, you must come back with us," Brother Gilbert pleaded, "You look in desperate need of rest."

"I'm sorry, Brother," Adelina said for the third time, "I can't."

"If you insist on being difficult, then promise you'll head west, toward the priory," Brother Gilbert pressed, his voice filled with concern, "They'll see you taken care of. 'Tis atop a hill, you can't miss it. If you run into the Firth, keep going west."

Adelina nodded, not entirely certain she'd remember anything he said. She bid them farewell, sternly ordering him not to tell anyone he'd seen her. Especially Ronan.

'Twas several hours more, and all she could think of was Ronan. She felt badly about leaving him, not knowing whether she lived or perished. And yet even if he had seen her leave, or happened upon her later, Adelina could never go back. If Ronan was finished with her, then she was finished with him.

By midmorning she'd been taken in by the kindly women just before passing out from exhaustion. She'd been sleeping ever since.

Chapter Thirty-Two

The words didn't register with Ronan right away. He went back to his work for a full minute before he realized what Brother Gilbert was implying.

"What?" he asked, hardly daring to hope.

Brother Gilbert smiled. "Aye, the wall fell upon her, and you didn't save her," he explained, "She saved herself. And left as quick as she could. We intercepted her on her way out of Calder lands."

Hope welled up inside Ronan. Could it be true? He rushed over to Brother Gilbert. "Where? Where did she go?"

"She didn't have a plan, other than to get far from Calder," Brother Gilbert continued, "I suggested she pay a visit to the sisters who live between here and my priory. I'd look there, were it me."

Shame rose hot as Ronan realized that she wasn't running from the fire. She was running from him. Because, as Brother Gilbert so tactfully pointed out, he was a coward. Ronan hugged Brother Gilbert for the first time since he'd been a lad. Then he ran to find his father.

Murdoch Calder was being cared for in one of the only cottages to survive the fire. Along with other injured clansmen, Murdoch spent his time convalescing on a cot. Lady Sybilla and the injured women were in the cottage next door.

Ronan had visited them both early that morn, to see them settled before he set to work rebuilding the village. When he'd left them, Lady Sybilla had still been unconscious, but her bleeding had finally stopped. His father had just woken, and was lucid enough to recognize Ronan and say a few words. He'd fallen back to sleep moments later.

Upon entering the small, one-room cottage, Ronan was surrounded by the smell of illness. The tang of blood hung in the air, a constant reminder of the pain endured by all in the room. The scent of healing herbs came as an afterthought, lightening the air only enough to render it bearable. Linens, both clean and covered in dried blood, littered the room. Buckets of water sat in a line just outside the door, easily accessible throughout the day to the women who frantically tried to keep up with the arduous task of caring for the injured.

Ronan would have much preferred privacy for this conversation, but there was no way around it. Luckily many of the clansmen were resting. He approached his father's cot carefully, so as not to wake him if he were resting. Ronan had seen the burns on his legs and back. When his father woke, he was likely to be in unbearable pain.

The fire had taken much of the spite from him, as far as Ronan could tell. Perhaps 'twas being rescued by a woman he'd wronged, or perhaps 'twas nearly losing his life twice over. Mayhap he was glad to be relieved of the responsibility of leading his clan. Either way, for the time being Murdoch Calder seemed simply happy to be alive.

Murdoch smiled as his son approached the bedside. "Hello, laird," he said, attempting a smile.

Ronan smiled back at him. "You're still the laird, father," Ronan reminded him.

"Nay," his father said hastily, "I'm hardly able to sit in my bed, let alone lead the clan. They need strength now. They need you."

Ronan couldn't find any words to respond to his father. The multitude of emotions that welled within him went far beyond speech. Angry and grateful, resentful and worried, overwhelmed and loved. His father had never been one for such talk, so Ronan simply placed a hand on his father's shoulder. No words were needed.

"If you don't mind, lad, I'm in need of some rest," Murdoch said gruffly.

"There was one other thing I had hoped to discuss, if you can," Ronan added. "I don't want to marry Lady Sybilla," he said gently.

His father made a movement that Ronan interpreted as a nod. "How is she?" he asked. 'Twas the most he'd spoken all day, and Ronan could see how it pained him.

"She lost a lot blood from the stab wound," he answered, "no one's certain whether she'll live the week out."

"Stab wound?" Murdoch said, "No, not Lady Sybilla. How is Adelina? Did she survive the fall?"

Ronan nearly laughed. His crotchety father was worried over Adelina. He must have fallen harder than Ronan realized. "Aye, she lives," he answered softly.

His father watched him for a moment. "Your face," he observed, "it changes when you speak of her. I never noticed it before."

"I love her."

Murdoch sighed, an effort that caused him to cough and then grimace. "I understand it now," he wheezed, "She's a fighter."

A smile caught Ronan by surprise. Never had he imagined his father capable of such a compliment for a woman, let alone one from whom he had once drawn personal insult. "I'm going to marry her," he stated.

"I certainly hope so," his father replied. Another fit of coughing came on, and Ronan called for water to help calm the spasm. A few swallows, and he had regained control of himself. He looked utterly exhausted.

Ronan said his farewell, explaining he might be gone for a day or so, and then left his father to get some rest. As he stepped out of the cottage, intending to make haste toward his horse, he heard Lady Sybilla's fragile voice inside the next cottage over. Fintan stepped out, nearly running into Ronan.

Ronan raised an eyebrow at him. Fintan had been spending an excess of time near the healing cottages.

"The lady requested an update on yesterday's events," he told Ronan. "Though I haven't mentioned your father or the collapse of the keep yet."

Ronan nodded. If he didn't know any better, he'd think Fintan was taken with the woman. Without another word, Ronan ducked inside. He hadn't the faintest idea what he would say to her. "I'm sorry you were stabbed" didn't seem quite right, and "I won't be marrying you" seemed plain cruel, given her current situation. Still, he knew something needed saying.

The beds for the women stood in rows, so that each had enough space to get up and down and have a visitor nearby. Lady Sybilla's bed was next to the largest window, in the front of the cottage. Her skin was so pale Ronan could nearly see through it.

Lord Blakewell, Lady Sybilla's father, sat nearby. He hadn't left her side since she'd been brought into the cottage. Throughout their stay at the keep, Lord Blakewell had been oddly quiet, keeping to himself and letting his daughter handle the social interactions between families. As a result, Ronan didn't know much of the man. He did respect Lord Blakewell's dedication to his daughter, however.

"Ronan," Lady Sybilla greeted him. Even speaking his name seemed to make her weary.

"'Tis good to see you awake and speaking, my lady," Ronan said, gracing her with the cheeriest smile he could manage.

"Did she live?" Lady Sybilla asked, her eyes full of concern. "Your father?"

Ronan nodded. "Both lived," he assured her.

Lady Sybilla smiled weakly. "Can I speak with her?"

"She left," Ronan informed her.

"Because of me?" she questioned.

"Nay, lass," he answered, looking her in the eyes, "because of me."

Lady Sybilla nodded, going silent for a moment. "I can't marry you, Ronan," she whispered, too weak to speak any louder. "I can't live here after what my maid has done to your clan. I'd never be welcome. And more than that, I couldn't marry a man who's heart was with another woman. I know it's silly for a noblewoman to say, a girlish fancy really. But I'd rather marry a man who's at least interested in learning to love one another."

"I understand," he answered softly. "I'm sorry I couldn't give that to you. Truly, I am." He gently squeezed her hand, then turned to leave.

"We will see justice done on behalf of your clan, laird," Lord Blakewell said, "You have my oath. We brought this destruction to you. We will make it right."

Ronan didn't doubt for a moment the sincerity of his vow. Motivated by grief, a man as powerful as Lord Blakewell could indeed seek vengeance with success. "I hope you'll stay with us while Lady Sybilla heals," Ronan said.

He wasn't yet prepared to discuss plans for justice, though he knew they were coming. Right now, he needed to find Adelina. Once he had her back, he could take on the world, and certainly one bloodthirsty rebel.

Lord Blakewell looked like he might burst into tears. He nodded, looking toward the ground. "Aye, laird, I'm afraid she can't be moved safely. 'Twill likely be a long while before she can make the journey home."

A sudden burst of sympathy drove Ronan to put a hand on the man's shoulder. "We'll do everything we can to see that she does," he said, trying to sound encouraging, and giving Lady Sybilla a smile so she wouldn't fret over her father's obvious distress.

Ronan had seen warriors twice her size lose as much blood and never recover. He prayed 'twas different for Lady Sybilla, but he wouldn't have wagered in her favor.

Finally taking his leave, Ronan made his way through the remains of the village to the burned-out shell of the stables. The horses had been brought back in and tied to makeshift posts. Several hadn't been recovered yet, but Ronan had sent some boys out looking 'round the clan lands. Sólas stomped impatiently as Ronan approached. Normally they rode every day, but with all that had been going on, Ronan had sorely neglected his old friend. He was overdue for a ride.

Nothing lifted his spirits like flying across the Highland's hills, soaring on his horse. The chill in the air cut through his exhaustion, and before he'd caught sight of the first loch Ronan knew he would find her. He would find her, and he would convince her to come back with him, to be his lass forever. He hadn't a clue what he'd say to accomplish such a thing, but he had the entire ride to figure it out. He spurred Sólas on, his heart racing as each minute brought him closer to Adelina.

Chapter Thirty-Three

When finally she woke, everything hurt. Adelina could hardly move her arms and legs, and when she worked up the courage to do so she felt as though fire ran the length of her insides. She grimaced as she pulled herself upright in the tidy cot. Taking a deep, shuddering breath, Adelina stood. And then fell back in the bed.

She let out a very unladylike groan and smacked the cot with her arms, which made them hurt even more. She whimpered, feeling rather sorry for herself.

"Having a bit of a morning, I see," Sister Cecilia observed lightly. She walked into the room and set down a tray on the nightstand. "A wee bite should help."

Adelina pushed herself up to a sitting position again with a groan. She could smell the warm bread from across the room. A bright red apple taunted her, tucked up against the bread. When she saw a pitcher of clear water, she realized that her mouth was so dry her lips were cracking. 'Twas all the motivation she needed to urge her sore muscles to action, albeit slowly.

Sister Cecilia watched her, likely making sure she didn't land flat on the floor in her current state. While Adelina gulped down water straight from the pitcher, Sister Cecilia placed a plain linen dress on the bed.

"If you're able to change," she said, "we can wash that for you. If you need help, call." She left Adelina to her breakfast, quietly shutting the door behind her.

Sister Cecilia, who had helped her into bed hours ago, had been right. After her breakfast, Adelina felt greatly improved. She stretched her aching body, knowing that as much as it pained her to move, 'twas the only way she would heal.

With much care, she changed her dress. She looked at it, wondering if 'twas even worth the effort of washing. Covered in blood, soot, and mud, torn in numerous places, Adelina deemed it beyond salvation, even for a nun. She left it in a pile atop the bed. 'Twould make a fine addition to her fire that night.

When she entered the small central hall of the priory, Adelina was surrounded by a dozen concerned nuns. Given their reception of her, Adelina thought they must not get many visitors. Sister Cecilia clapped her hands, commanding everyone's attention.

"Adelina needs air," she ordered, "Have a walk out in the garden, my dear. It'll do you a world of good." She walked over to Adelina and wrapped a woolen blanket about her shoulders, then turned her in the direction of the garden.

Though Adelina felt like she hadn't much choice in the matter, a bit of fresh air did sound appealing. And a priory garden, notoriously well tended, held great promise. Adelina found herself hurrying out the door.

'Twas indeed lovely. Adelina strolled the perfectly manicured pathways, running her hands along the rows of fragrant herbs as she went. Lavender, chamomile, thyme, mint. Comfrey, calendula, St. John's wort. Rose bushes were flush with pink and red flowers, their last display before winter set in. A beehive was just waking. Sleepy buzzing gained momentum as its inhabitants stirred.

Adelina breathed deeply in the tranquility of the place. She could stay here forever in this quiet piece of paradise. But what would she actually do? Brother Gilbert had told her to come here, regain her strength, and make a plan. But a plan for what? Had she not burned all her bridges last night?

She had pushed away Ronan with her demands. If she hadn't allowed her feelings to interfere with her judgment, they might have stopped the fire. She'd been so obsessed with winning Ronan's affection, so worried over his marriage to Lady Sybilla, that she hadn't taken time to properly consider the situation. She'd wanted Lady Sybilla out of the picture, by way of her own guilt, so badly that she couldn't consider any alternative. When she finally did, it was too late.

Aye, she had let her emotions command her actions, and an entire village had burned for it. She was a fool for ever believing someone like Ronan could love her. She certainly shouldn't be cross with him for pointing out that she was, in fact, of common birth. 'Twas the truth, and an important consideration for marriage.

She wouldn't be getting her letter into Oxford now, and she didn't deserve it anyway. She'd been an absolute fool, run away with her emotions. Her father and brother would always welcome her back, but she couldn't face them with only failure to her name. What could she do?

Adelina made her way to a stone bench to think. As soon as she'd sat down on its cold surface, hoof beats sounded in the distance. It put her in mind of a day not so very long ago, when Ronan had caught her wandering alone. She stood, squinting to see who approached the small priory. Then her breath caught in her throat. Her heart quickened in her chest. 'Twas Ronan, riding straight for her.

Her heart thudded heavily in her chest, but alongside it a sinking feeling grew in her middle. The last time he'd come for her, furious and distant, he'd shouted at her for her foolishness. Had he come to do the same? Mayhap he blamed her for the fire or for his father's injuries. Why else would he have come so far? He must be here to seek retribution for her great crimes against his clan.

As he neared, she saw the serious look on his face. A glorious shade of brown-green, his eyes never left her as he jumped from Sólas. He was in such a hurry, the great beast had hardly stopped moving before Ronan flew from his back, running straight for Adelina. She braced herself, knowing she deserved what was coming.

When he reached her, he threw his arms around her so tightly she could hardly breathe. He squeezed her with all his strength, lifting her until her feet were off the ground. He said not a word.

Adelina was speechless at first. She'd expected many things. Shouting, anger, sadness, frustration, despair, pain, grief – the list went on. She had not expected a hug so intense it might have killed her. "Ronan," she wheezed.

He lessened his grip on her, but only just.

She inhaled deeply. "What is going on?" she asked in shock.

He lowered her to the ground, moving his hands to cup her face. Ronan stared deeply into her eyes, his gaze burning with intensity. "I love you."

Adelina didn't have even a moment to reply. His lips were on hers, a desperate, deep kiss. She could feel how much he needed it, and it only confused her the more. Adelina pulled back enough to look at him.

"I don't understand," she stammered. "What about my common birth? Lady Sybilla?"

Ronan took her hands in his. "I always loved you," he replied, "I never wanted anyone else. Especially Lady Sybilla," he added, almost an afterthought. "I was too much of a coward to marry you. I was so terrified that you would die in childbirth, and I would have to live without you. The only way to save you was to leave you, and I knew you'd never believe such a ridiculous reason."

Confusion warred with hope inside Adelina. She wasn't exactly certain she understood what he'd said, but she knew he was pouring his heart out to her and she wasn't about to interrupt. Could he be saying that he wanted to be with her? She sighed, realizing how much that would be asking of him.

"But then you died," he said, continuing his explanation, "or at least I thought you did, and I realized none of it mattered. I realized I could lose you in a thousand ways, but the only mistake I could ever make would be leaving you to face them alone."

Adelina's heart raced. She ran her hand along his cheek, admiring the strong lines of his jaw, his wild, dark hair. "You rode all the way here to tell me you loved me?" she asked.

"Nay, lass," he replied, pulling her close to him once more, "I rode all the way here to make you mine. I want you to come back to Calder. I want you to marry me." He paused, kissing her tenderly. "I want you for the rest of my life," he whispered.

Adelina threw her arms about his neck. She answered him with a kiss passionate enough to match his own. They stood there, drinking each other in, holding each other so close that Adelina forgot the cold. She forgot the day, the time, and everything else for that matter. She had all that she needed. She had Ronan.

Chapter Thirty-Four

By midafternoon, Adelina and Ronan arrived back at the ruins of the keep. Aside from towers of flame and smoke, the world had been shrouded in darkness when Adelina left the night before, making it easy to overlook the extent of the destruction. She gazed about the wasteland before her. Where once there had been a grand keep nestled in a charming village, now there stood piles of rubble as high as the hills.

The smell of char assaulted her nostrils as they rode to a burned out shell of a building. 'Twas once the stables, Adelina realized. Dismounting in a daze, she spun slowly. She'd never seen such disaster.

"How on earth will we to fix it?" she wondered aloud.

Ronan turned from tethering the horses to look at her. "Together," he answered.

Adelina appreciated the notion that together they might rebuild a clan, but her eyes told her it would not be as easy as it sounded. Where to even begin? Rubble covered so much of the land, there was hardly a spot in which to build anew.

"Don't worry over it, lass," he said, walking up behind her and wrapping her in his arms, "I've a plan for the buildings. 'Twill take time, aye, but 'twill get done. Right now, the people need you."

Adelina spun around to face him, realization dawning on her. "Your father! I can't believe I forgot. Where is he?"

Ronan's eyes saddened. "You'll need your things," he told her, "and 'tis not only my father."

Adelina hurried in the direction of her cottage. "What do you mean?" she asked, "Are there many who were injured?"

"Only nine were injured, some not terribly. The worst injury was not my father's, though. 'Twas Lady Sybilla's."

Adelina stopped instantly. "What happened? Why didn't you say something earlier?"

Ronan kept walking, gently tugging on her arm to hurry her along. "What could you have done while you were miles away?" he reasoned, "I didn't want you to worry over it until you could take action. Lucy stabbed her."

Adelina felt the blood fall from her face. It ended up somewhere near her toes. Lord, she hadn't a clue how to treat an injury like that. She certainly didn't have the right herbs for it.

"What is it?" Ronan asked.

"We need Gemma," Adelina said, now running toward her cottage.

Ronan kept pace with her, his brows furrowing. "You can't treat her?"

Adelina shrugged. "I can try," she said, "but I'm still learning. I don't know the first thing about a wound from a sword or dagger. I learned about coughs and scratches, agues and fevers. A bit of burns, but nothing so serious as this. We need a real healer."

Ronan let out a groan, and Adelina took exception to that.

"It'll be alright," she said, "I can still help. But," she started to explain.

"'Tis not that, lass," he interrupted her, pointing toward the ruins that were once her cottage.

"No!" Adelina sprinted over top of what had been her roof. Her hands ran through her hair, as though by pulling on it she could think faster. All her jars were a mess upon the cottage floor. Most of her herbs were burned to ash. Tears threatened as panic gripped her. She had nothing, no salves, no herbs. No way to help all those people who were injured. No way to heal Murdoch or Lady Sybilla.

Ronan turned her to face him, holding her shoulders tightly. "Adelina," he said in a firm voice, "what grows here that you can use?"

She ran her hand over her face, pulling on her chin before dropping it to her waist. "Nothing," she replied. "The garden is nearly barren, and now it's surely naught but ash."

Her mind raced. She couldn't simply give up. But what could she possibly use? Then it struck her, an idea so simple it was clearly the only option. She had just read it in the herbal a few days past. "How much garlic do you have?" she asked.

Ronan smiled. He dragged her toward the outer cottages, the ones that were still mostly intact. Mayhap Adelina could heal them after all.

An hour later, Adelina entered the first healing cottage, mixture in hand. She could smell the herbs the women had been using, lavender and chamomile for certain. The air held a sweetness that hinted at honey. Likely they used it to soothe burned skin. Adelina also caught a whiff of something stronger. Whiskey. Were they cleansing the wounds with it? As she walked over to Murdoch's cot, she realized 'twas he who smelled of drink.

"Lass," he said, his speech slurred, "I owe you my life. I know I underestimated you, and I'll pay my debts."

Adelina wasn't certain he'd remember saying any such thing once the alcohol wore off. She smiled anyway, happy he was able to hold conversation at all. At least her efforts hadn't been for naught.

"I need to look at your legs," she told him, "Hold as still as you can."

He nodded, and she peeled back the bandages. It took all her presence of mind not to gasp at the extent of his burns. It was immediately clear that he drank to dull the pain of them. She knew his skin needed to stay cool and clean. After she replaced the bandages, she looked at him sternly.

"I know the whiskey helps with your pain," she said, "but you won't be drinking any more of it."

Murdoch began muttering his opposition to that statement, but Adelina held up her hand.

"It will only make it more difficult to heal," she said, "You'll be drinking water and willow bark, and I can add herbs to help you sleep as well should you desire them."

He grumbled at her ordering him about. Ronan stayed to speak with him on some matter, and Adelina walked next door to where the women were recovering. She took a deep breath before going inside, knowing that Lady Sybilla would be in a sorry state.

Ronan had explained to her what had happened as she made her garlic mixture, making certain Adelina knew that Lady Sybilla had lost quite a lot of blood. 'Twas the truth that made her even more anxious, for she knew nothing of such treatments.

Inside, she found Lady Sybilla propped upright in her cot against several pillows. Her father sat beside her, holding her hand. He was a picture of concern. Lady Sybilla was pale as a ghost, her eyes dull and sunken. It pained Adelina to see her so sickly and not know how to help her. She supposed her poor father must feel similarly.

"Sybilla," Adelina said gently, walking to stand next to her father, "I'm glad to see you awake. How are you feeling?"

Lady Sybilla smiled at her. "I've felt better," she replied. Then she grimaced and her hand went to her side, ruining her attempt at levity.

"May I take a look?" Adelina asked, stepping closer as Lord Blakewell moved out of the way. "Have you been able to eat anything?"

Lady Sybilla shook her head. "No," she answered, "I've no appetite. Truth be told I feel quite off."

Adelina nodded. 'Twas no more than she'd expect after suffering so grave an injury. Lady Sybilla was lucky to be alive. She'd be even luckier if they kept her that way.

The bandages had a good deal of dried blood, but the wound appeared to have stopped bleeding. Adelina let out a sigh of relief. One good sign, at least. 'Twas a dreadfully deep cut, though, and even if Lady Sybilla regained her strength, she was at risk of fever if the wound closed poorly. But Adelina wasn't about to tell her that. Causing her worry wouldn't help her to heal.

"You're awfully quiet," Lady Sybilla observed, "Is something wrong? Does it look bad?"

Adelina chuckled, trying to keep spirits high. "It looks like you were stabbed, my lady. I'll need to clean it again, and wrap it in a new bandage. I've brought a mixture that should help it to heal, but I'll warn you – it smells like hell."

"What's in it?" Lord Blakewell asked, curiously eyeing the bowl Adelina held.

"'Tis probably better if you don't know," she answered truthfully. She called over one of the women, whom she learned was named Anna, and sent her to get a small plate of simple fare and broth for the lady.

Lady Sybilla objected. "I don't believe I could eat a thing," she said.

"You've lost too much blood," Adelina explained calmly, "I'll tell you now that I don't know much about that particular ailment, but I do know one thing. Blood is your strength, and you've lost it. Food gives you strength, and 'tis the only way I can think of for you to regain what you've lost. Eat what you can, as often as you can. Even drinking the broth will help." Adelina prayed that was true, for without Gemma she had no way of knowing what to do.

Lady Sybilla nodded. Adelina began the arduous task of cleaning and redressing her wound. She worked as quickly as she could, knowing how greatly it pained Lady Sybilla. After sitting through the washing with her lips pressed together like a vice, the delicate lady passed out from the pain. Adelina sighed in relief. It would be easier for everyone. She hurried to apply the mixture she'd brought and wrap the wound in a clean linen.

By the time she'd finished, the strong smell of the garlic had roused Lady Sybilla. She laid silently, watching Adelina clean up her materials. Ronan walked in, another man behind him. Of a similar height and build, the man had longer, curlier hair and piercing blue eyes. They could have been brothers.

"Adelina, this is Aidan, my cousin."

Adelina dropped the bandages she'd been packing away. "Aidan? As in the Aidan who wrote the letter?"

Ronan chuckled. "Aye, the very same."

"'Tis a pleasure to meet you, lass." Aidan's voice was deeper than Ronan's, and louder.

Adelina strode toward Aidan, pointing her finger at him accusingly. "What in the world were you thinking?" Adelina asked.

Aidan frowned at her. "I beg your pardon?"

"Your letter," she said. "Why on earth would you make the most important line impossible to read? It took me until Samhain Eve to decipher the blasted thing. And what good did it do me by then?"

"Apparently trying to save your lives wasn't enough, then," Aidan replied. "If you must know, I was worried that my messenger would be followed. A fear, I might add, that proved well founded. Hoping that even if he were caught, you might still get the letter, I encoded the end in the simplest way I could devise. Only someone well versed in Latin could figure it out, meaning one of those uneducated zealots might pass it along without understanding its significance."

"Zealots? There are more of them?" Ronan asked. He looked none too happy over it.

"A castle full, at least," Aidan answered. "They're harboring Malcolm in the hopes of putting him back on the throne."

"Not for long they aren't." Lord Blakewell's tenor voice sounded from behind them. He and Lady Sybilla had been listening quietly to the conversation. "I'll see to it they are held accountable for their crimes."

"As will we," Ronan vowed. "For now, let's leave Lady Sybilla to get her rest."

Ronan and Aidan bid them farewell and left the cottage, deep in conversation about rebels and rebuilding.

Lady Sybilla looked at Adelina after they'd gone. "Where did you learn to do that?" she asked in awe. "To mix such a potion and apply it so skillfully? To know whether I should eat or abstain?"

Adelina swallowed hard. She felt she knew nothing for certain. 'Twas all a guess from the books she'd read with Gemma and the knowledge she'd gained working alongside her friend. She'd never risked someone's life with her knowledge. Until now.

"I lived at Oxford, before I came here," Adelina began, not entirely certain where she was going, "My brother was a student, and I had been trying to be allowed to study with him. I met a woman one day who was a masterful healer, but her Latin was wanting. She and I read through the medical guides in the library together, and she taught me many things. But my knowledge is nothing in comparison with her own. I was only her student."

Lady Sybilla nodded, her eyes narrowed. She considered Adelina for a long moment. "Did they allow you entry?" she asked at last, "To the lectures?"

Adelina choked out a laugh. If only. "No," she replied, "They sent me here and dangled my acceptance as reward for a thankless task."

"Master Gregory is my uncle," Lady Sybilla said with a weak grin. "I'll see you accepted by month's end."

"Sybilla," Adelina started in, not wanting to cause undue trouble.

"I won't hear otherwise," she said firmly, "'Tis the very least I can do after the catastrophe that has been the last two days."

Before Adelina could find the words to thank her, Lady Sybilla had grown too drowsy to continue to conversation. Adelina left in a stupor, trying to make sense of all that had happened since she woke yesterday morn. She simply couldn't. Instead, she allowed herself a grin, as though she were telling Gemma the good news. It looked like she'd be the first woman into Oxford after all.

CHAPTER THIRTY-FIVE

December 2, 1136

One month later, Ronan and Adelina arrived outside an ostentatious townhouse in the bustling city of Oxford. In England. Ronan had never imagined a day when he would set foot so far to the south, let alone by his own free will. And yet, he could hardly wait to meet Adelina's family. She'd been talking about them for almost twenty days now, so he felt as though he knew them already.

Adelina had originally suggested that they marry on Yule, as many folk did. It would give her kin enough time to attend if they sent for them right away. Ronan had bristled at that. He had put off marriage his entire adult life thus far, and now that he was committed, he could hardly wait. And he certainly couldn't wait two months.

Instead, Ronan had convinced Adelina that they should carry the message in person and be married as soon as possible thereafter. She insisted on sending a letter several days ahead so that her father wasn't taken completely by surprise, and three weeks after Samhain, they were en route to Oxford.

Ronan's main concern at rushing the wedding and their travels out of Calder was the welfare of his clan. He didn't want to abandon them at a crucial moment, and, though he chafed at the very thought, he had been prepared to postpone the wedding until the clan could handle his absence.

After three weeks of constant building, thatching, and shifting, every person in Clan Calder had a home for the winter. They were nowhere near finished with rebuilding yet, but everyone had what they needed for the time being. Ronan had left John, Lowrance, and Alan in charge of overseeing the continued construction, with strict orders to send him word of any pressing matters.

Ronan's secondary concern after his clan was Adelina's safety on the dangerous journey through a war-torn Borderland. Aidan and his men, Ross and Gordon, accompanied Ronan and Adelina all the way to Oxford as added protection. Ronan knew he was lucky to have such loyal kinsmen.

Just as a groom appeared to collect their horses, the front door of the townhouse burst open.

Jocelin Matheson, with hair to match his sister's fiery locks, ran straight for Adelina and picked her up into his arms. Ronan watched with fascination.

"Lord, but I've worried over you," he whispered as he squeezed the life from her.

"I've been more worried over your studies," she teased. "How is Cicero?"

"Dead, thankfully," Jocelin said with distaste. "I hope I never meet the bastard again."

Her father took that opportunity to step forward, embracing her in a far more dignified fashion. "'Tis a pleasure to see you, love," he greeted her warmly.

Adelina threw her arms about her father's neck.

Adelina was so overjoyed, Ronan thought she might start dancing. Her feet wouldn't stop moving, and a breathtaking smile had taken up permanent residence on her face. Ronan cleared his throat, drawing Adelina's attention so that he could finally be introduced.

"Oh! I'm sorry," she apologized, "Ronan, this is my father, Henry Matheson, and my brother, Jocelin."

Her father offered his arm to Ronan in greeting as Adelina still spoke, and a smile with it. "We are glad to have you as family," he said sincerely.

"I'm grateful for your allowing Adelina to stay with us," Ronan replied, "I know 'tis not easy to let her go."

Jocelin also offered his arm to Ronan in turn, but he was more skeptical. "We'll see," was all he said.

Ronan grinned at him, utterly unshaken. "Aye," he replied, "we will."

Two days later, on the morning of his wedding, Ronan woke with a start. Adelina was nowhere to be found, and light streamed through the nearby window. How could he have missed the sunrise? He never overslept.

Launching himself from the cot, Ronan fumbled about the room for his plaid and the finest linen shirt he owned. He wore an outfit so fitting of a Highlander that even Alan, the fastidious clan elder, would have been proud.

Henry had been blessedly accommodating. Ronan spoke with him the night of their arrival about getting the wedding underway with all haste. He had expected at least some hesitation from Adelina's father, but he seemed just as overjoyed as his daughter. With impeccable diplomacy, Henry noted that given the political situation it would be better to make the wedding an intimate affair anyway. They would send for the priest and make a few decorative arrangements.

Jocelin caught up with Ronan as he entered the dining hall. The room was half the size of the one Calder Keep used to have, but far more extravagant. Ornate wood carvings adorned every surface imaginable. Gold and gemstone inlays graced so much of the décor, it looked as though they had fallen like rain about the room. The chairs had cushions. *Cushions.* Ronan's father would be laughing himself to death at such nonsense.

"Better hurry up," Jocelin said, "Won't want to keep Addi waiting."

Ronan nearly choked on the boiled egg he had started to swallow. "Addi?"

"I've always called her that," Jocelin explained, shooting him a cheeky grin. "What? She didn't tell you to call her by her nickname?"

Ronan knew Jocelin was testing him, so he smiled as he finished chewing. "Oh, I call her by a nickname," Ronan said, keeping his face serious with great effort, "but 'tis quite a different one." Then he winked at Jocelin.

Now 'twas Jocelin's turn to balk. Before he could manage a reply, Henry walked into the room.

"You lads had better hurry it up," he warned, "the priest has to be somewhere by midday."

Jocelin left immediately. Ronan finished a few bites of porridge before he followed. He grudgingly admitted to himself that the cushions were comfortable, but no less ridiculous.

The small garden behind the Matheson townhouse had been utterly transformed. Boughs of pine, fir, and holly decorated a small courtyard. Lanterns had been placed in alcoves, protected from the angry winds, flickering a joyful dance. Garlands of dried lavender hung from pillars of stone. Dried rose petals covered the ground, their flowery scent wafting gently into the air every time they were crushed underfoot. A light snow fell, and it dusted everything in a soft glimmer of white.

While Ronan admired the beautiful setting and appreciated the care that so many had clearly put into it, he couldn't keep his eyes off Adelina. She wore a sapphire blue gown of some of the finest fabric he'd ever seen. And her hair was down. It fell in waves of fire across her shoulders, adorned with cascades of pearls and creamy flowers. She was a vision. She was his vision.

Ronan fought the urge to take her into his arms, carry her off, and be done with it. He told her he would marry her, and by God he would do it properly. Instead, with a great feat of patience, he walked slowly to where she waited with the priest. When at last he reached her, Ronan took her hands in his.

The priest began the ceremony promptly. He didn't mince words, and he didn't waste any time. Jocelin handed the priest a cloth. He wrapped it around Ronan and Adelina's hands, binding them together.

"'Tis time for the vows," he declared. "Adelina, you'll go first."

Adelina nodded her understanding.

"Do you promise to be a good and true wife, to care for Ronan through all life's many trials, and to love him and honor him all the days of your life?"

"Aye, I do," Adelina vowed, her eyes never straying from Ronan's.

"Ronan," the priest continued, "do you promise to be a good and true husband, to care for Adelina through all life's many trials, and to love and honor her all the days of your life?"

Hearing the words, anxiety rushed through Ronan. All the fears he had carried throughout his life struck him in one final moment.

Adelina sensed his change in mood instantly. She ran her hand along his scruffy cheek, her eyes full of understanding.

Ronan took a deep breath. The thought of marrying Adelina, of having this companionship for the rest of his life, calmed his worry. Everything would be fine as long as they were together. They had already faced so many challenges, Ronan knew whatever was thrown at them would pass.

Ronan looked her in the eyes, searching her face. Then he smiled. "Aye, lass," he vowed, "I do."

EPILOGUE

December 13, 1136

Where on earth was he? Adelina paced atop the staircase. Back and forth, over and over, until she was certain he had forgotten. If he didn't get here soon, they would be late. She had been waiting just outside the front door for an agonizing ten minutes. Maybe even a quarter hour.

Out of the corner of her eye, she saw Ronan approach the bottom of the stairs. He leaned against the corner of the stable wall, arms crossed.

"Well it's about time, laird," she said crossly.

He strode up the stairs, two at a time, and lifted her into his arms. "Quit your fretting, lass," he ordered, easily maneuvering back to the ground, "'Tis going to be a glorious day, whether you worry or not."

Adelina sighed, letting her head rest on his strong chest. Lord, was she ever lucky to have such a man. She didn't care a whit whether it was proper or not to be so close in public. "Fine," she agreed, snuggling against him, "I'll stop fretting. But can we please go now?"

Ronan chuckled, then nodded, setting her gently back on her own two feet. "Lead the way," he proclaimed, gesturing grandly before them.

They walked hand-in-hand through the streets of Oxford. Many of the main thoroughfares were paved, as wealth poured into the city by means of both the university and trade. The rich spent time here, so the city was kept better than most. Though fewer flowers were in bloom in the winter months, the citrusy smell of spruce boughs followed them the entire journey. Holly and ivy decorated many a building.

Time slowed as they approached their destination. Adelina's breath came in quick spurts, and she worried for a moment she might actually cry.

Ronan turned to her, stroking her jaw line with his thumb and smiling warmly. "'Twill be alright, *mo chridhe*," he whispered, pulling her in for a hug.

Adelina nodded into his warm chest, then pulled away. She had to be going or she'd be late. And that simply wouldn't do. After inhaling and exhaling several times, she regained her composure.

"Thank you," she whispered back, turning to face the dark-timbered building.

Then Adelina pulled open an ornate oak door and walked into the lecture hall at Oxford.

If you loved Adelina & Ronan's story, please consider leaving a review on Amazon, Goodreads, or BookBub.

Want More?

I've got you covered. Here are all the ways you can get more content:

Grab A Wild Winter on Amazon.

Gemma and Aidan's adventure has only begun. Join them as they trek through the snowy English countryside in A Wild Winter.

Subscribe to my newsletter.

You'll get a free novella (To Love A Laird), as well as exclusive content, updates, and so many freebies! Sign up here: https://landing.mailerlite.com/webforms/landing/x2wlg7

Follow me on social media.

Let's be friends! Follow me for all sorts of shenanigans, including really embarrassing photos.

@SophiaNyeWrites

sophianyewrites.com

Le gaol,

Sophia

Can a fiery, runaway princess melt a wandering warrior's heart?

All she wants is to disappear...
Gemma FitzRoy, illegitimate daughter of King Henry and a Welsh princess, finds herself standing face to face with her worst nightmare: an arranged marriage to a monster of a man. After an unpleasant encounter with her would-be betrothed, Gemma takes off into the wilderness in search of a new future. When she stumbles into an uncooperative Highlander, Gemma must take drastic action to ensure he doesn't place her into danger unwittingly.

All he wants is to keep her safe...
Aidan MacMaster has never felt at home in his Highland clan. Always on the lookout for excuses to leave his family in search of adventure, Aidan gets more than he bargained for when he agrees to go off in search of a missing woman. 'Twould be a far easier task if the lass would stop fighting him at every turn in the road.

Together, they must decide what it means to go home.
Swept away together on a journey of discovery and intrigue, Gemma and Aidan must decide between the pasts they left behind and the future they imagine together. Will one wild winter night together free them from the past or freeze their hearts forever?

Meet Sophia

A historian and archaeologist turned writer, Sophia has been making up stories since she could talk. When she isn't working on her next novel, you can find her in the garden. Sophia lives in Indiana with her husband, two children, and their menagerie of pets.

Hello, you!

I wanted to reach out and thank you for reading my book! Ever since I was a kid I've wanted to be a writer, and when you picked up this book, you helped to make that happen. I'm truly grateful that you decided to step into my reimagined medieval world. I hope that you enjoyed our time together.

I love to hear from readers. It always makes my day when someone takes the time to get in touch. Feel free to email me at sophia@sophianyewrites.com with any questions, comments, or to just say hello.

Warmest wishes,

Sophia

Made in United States
North Haven, CT
29 April 2024

51903711R00115